NO ONE BUT US

GREGORY SPATZ

NO ONE

·········

BUT US

·········

Algonquin Books of Chapel Hill / 1995

Published by
ALGONQUIN BOOKS OF CHAPEL HILL
Post Office Box 2225
Chapel Hill, North Carolina 27515-2225

a division of
WORKMAN PUBLISHING COMPANY, INC.
708 Broadway
New York, New York 10003

This is a work of fiction. Names, characters, places, and incidents are either the product of the author's imagination or are used fictitiously. Any resemblance to actual events or locales or persons, living or dead, is entirely coincidental.

Grateful acknowledgment is made to the *New England Review*, where chapter one of this novel appeared in slightly different form, entitled "My Mother, Jolene, and Me."

LIBRARY OF CONGRESS CATALOGING-IN-PUBLICATION DATA
Spatz, Gregory, 1964–
    No one but us / Gregory Spatz.
      p. cm.
    ISBN 1-56512-037-X
    I. Title.
    PS3569.P377N6   1995
    813'.54—dc20   95–18897
                                          CIP

10 9 8 7 5 4 3 2 1
First Edition

My thanks to Devon Jersild, Rob Odom, Robert Rubin, and Anne Dubuisson for their support, criticism, and help getting this book to light; thanks also to Ann Williams for many insightful readings; thanks to all my San Francisco Bay area music friends for musical inspiration, especially Rob Ickes and Alberto Vasquez who gave me a place to live; thanks to Kristin Steege for earliest motivation; and thanks to everyone in my family for their continued support. Most of all, love and thanks to my parents, Larry and Alice Spatz.

NO ONE BUT US

JOLENE

Jolene had been one of my mother's best friends for years. Some of my earliest recollections are of the two of them on long summer afternoons, sitting out in the backyard in their swimuits. We never had a pool, but that didn't stop them. They would drink and sweat. I remember they talked about what they wished for, and most of it had to do with money or men. Jolene was eight years younger than my mother and they liked to discuss her different possibilities. There were interruptions too—the phone, people coming over. I was always amazed at how fast they were able to pull themselves together when this happened. I couldn't put my finger on it, but I knew there was an effect they had on each other which had to remain separate from everything else in the world. It was a kind of softening or drunkenness. They talked about the world like it was with them there in the backyard and they could set it up or make it fall however they wanted.

Our lawn was more yellow than green and hardly ever needed mowing. It was small, about half an acre between

the pines that blocked our view of Mr. Chenille's backyard and house—which was exactly like ours, only
white—and the back steps leading inside our house. But
it got a lot of sun, and as long as there was sun Jolene
and my mother didn't act like they knew or cared where
they were.

The fall I turned fifteen my mother tried to kill herself, but she only managed to bruise her vocal cords and
break her leg. The break was a compound fracture in her
thigh that kept her in the hospital for over a month. All
that time I lived with Jolene.

I think Jolene was more upset when it happened than
I was. She was there waiting for me after school with half
my stuff piled in back of her car. I couldn't tell what upset
her more: the fact it had happened or what she thought I
must be going through when she told me about it. We
went straight to her place and then back to my mother's
when I pointed out that she had forgotten all my shirts.

There was police tape across our front door, and one of
the small windows next to the front picture window had
been smashed. Nobody ever said why. I remember thinking
things looked much worse than they probably were, like
this was the scene of some huge crime or accident, which I
understood it wasn't. Jolene insisted I shouldn't go inside.
She left the car idling and ran up the front steps, looking
both ways before she ducked under the tape.

The way Jolene had explained it, my mother didn't

think she was living up to things anymore. I wasn't sure I understood this. I knew how much my mother hated her job at the hospital, where she was a med tech. She said the work bored her. There was a time when she talked about going to school for another degree in chemistry, but it was never more than talk. She said she eventually realized that you can't hate the thing you love (meaning science) for too long without losing something—some of your faith or concern, she said. I also knew her marriage hadn't worked because the man she married was my father, and he had spent the last ten years floating around the Caribbean and the Mediterranean, cooking and tending bar on luxury liners. This was nothing new for me to hear about. I didn't understand what my mother thought she had to live up to all of a sudden.

Jolene said it had to do with her feeling older; that every day my mother lived was just another day none of the things she had hoped for and expected came about. That was why she wanted to kill herself. Jolene said it was that simple. I remember thinking it wasn't that simple at all, and at least half of the problem was that my mother really *didn't* know what she hoped for and expected out of life, beyond the fact that it should be somehow better than what she already had. But you don't point out the truth about someone who has barely survived killing herself.

I tried to see into the house after Jolene so I could

know what she wanted to protect me from. No more, I was thinking, no more. No more *what* I couldn't have said. I didn't understand that part of it, I just understood there would be no more. The boundaries between things would fall away and I would finally have the world as it really was.

When Jolene came back she dumped my shirts in my lap. They smelled like our house, like the soap we used and the food we ate, and for a second I was so scared I could barely see.

"She'd done all the laundry," Jolene said. "They were all right there, folded up and clean, like she must have had the whole damn thing planned. I don't know how I missed them the first time. They were right there." She thumped her hands on the steering wheel. Then she was going fifty-five down side roads I knew I wouldn't see again for some time.

I HAD been to Jolene's before, but not often. She lived in a modern apartment complex called The Aspens, which was close enough to school for me to walk in the mornings. The layout there made no sense to me for a while and I was always getting lost, turning off the wrong corridor and wandering through places nobody lived yet. There were three buildings joined like a hive, and many ways to get in and out of each of them. Once I had found a reliable, direct path I could usually remember—from the far back door to 3C, which was her number—I stuck with it. It didn't matter that I had to circle the building and go up an extra flight of stairs; I didn't want to get lost inside.

My first night there she made a lot of spaghetti for us. We sat next to each other at the counter dividing her living room and kitchen, not talking much. She had on a bathrobe because it was late and the first thing she had done when we got back from the hospital was to take a shower. I remember her sliding around the kitchen with her socks down around her ankles while she heated things up. Then, when she sat down she crossed one leg over the other and her robe fell aside so that I could see the place just above her knee where she stopped shaving, and the smooth skin all down her calf.

"You don't have to go to school for a few days, if you don't want," she said. Her eyes were light green with yellow through them. That night they seemed unusually light and shiny, more copper than green. "That's probably okay, right?" she asked.

"Fine with me."

"Of course it's fine with you. That's not what I meant." She gave me the kind of smile people use to pretend nothing is wrong. "I meant your mother might not want you out of school very long."

"Probably not."

"You're *not* taking advantage of this situation, Charlie."

"Probably not."

She glanced at her wrist, but she didn't have her watch on; then she squinted across the kitchen at the clock in the range top. "Mary's out of OR by now," she said. "What did they say, eight, nine o'clock? We should call."

"Mary, Mary, quite contrary," I said. We both said this sometimes to make fun of my mother when she was being difficult.

"I don't believe you!" She pinched my shoulder. "What did you just say? I don't believe it!" She tried to pinch me again but I got her by the fingers and held on.

"Don't even think about it," I said, because I saw she was eyeing her wineglass, measuring the distance between it and me, probably thinking she would like to pour it over my head. "Don't even try," I said.

Something went out of her. She shook her head and put her other hand on my shoulder. "Poor Charlie," she said.

There had always been a kind of playful side to the way Jolene and I got along. Once when she was drunk she kissed me. She might have forgotten about it, but I never did. It happened at the end of a day we had spent with my mother at Old Saybrook beach, swimming. I must have been about eleven. She was twenty-three. All the way back from Old Saybrook to Farmington Jolene had her arm around me. The three of us were in our suits in the front seat of my mother's station wagon and Jolene's breast was practically in my ear. I remember her making fun of me for being embarrassed about that; then she told me I should never grow up because I'd only turn out like other men.

"Assholes," my mother said. "All of them."

"There's a few good ones," Jolene said and tightened her hold on me. Then she slid down in the seat so we were on the same level and she looked at me. "Initiation time," she said. "Charlie, have you ever kissed a girl?"

"He hasn't," my mother said.

"How would you know? Have you?" she asked again. But before I could answer that yes, I had in fact kissed a girl once a year ago at someone's birthday party, she got me square on the mouth and pushed her tongue across my teeth. She smelled like sun and sweat and suntan lotion and she tasted like the vodka she'd been drinking all day. It was no interruption to her breathing and talking, the way she kissed me. It was just something to do. Her hair was in my mouth and all over my face. She only broke off when she started laughing too hard to keep her mouth on mine. Then my mother slapped her in back of the head and told her she was giving me fresh ideas. Jolene said just the opposite; now I wouldn't have to go around wondering what it was like all the time. For my part, I felt sleepy and overwhelmed, and relaxed in a peculiar way—too relaxed to say anything about it really, except, if she had offered, I might have said that I wished it would go on awhile longer.

Later there were food fights and tickling fights, but

never anything like what had happened on the way home from Old Saybrook. I used to try to make Jolene tell whether or not she might remember kissing me, or whether it was likely to happen again, but she ignored my efforts.

My mother had been out of OR for a while by the time Jolene got through. The nurses said she would be fine; they told Jolene again that it was a compound fracture but it wasn't terrible, and nothing had been damaged in my mother's neck. They said that right now she was asleep. Jolene was playing with her hair while she listened, spooling it around a finger then letting it straighten and drift over her hand. She kept her face turned away so I wouldn't see how close she was to crying, but I didn't have to see to know about that.

I slept on a cot under the low window in her spare room, but I didn't sleep much at first because of all the street noise and because of a light right outside the window that buzzed and flickered all night. I remember my first night there, lying on my back and looking down at myself under the covers, kicking my feet now and then just to change the shape of the light going over the blanket. I wished I had more ways to think about what was happening in my life. One thing I knew: I was glad to be there in her apartment, even though I knew I shouldn't be. This was possibly one of the worst nights of my life, and I ought to recognize that somehow. But everything was loose inside me. I didn't understand it. It seemed like my ideas about what had happened would shift and turn into something else every time I tried to make them clear or put a name on them like happy, sad, or scared, and I had a glowing feeling I couldn't control, as if the sun were right in my head. I ought to have been more upset than I was, but even knowing that gave me a kind of thrill. I knew I wouldn't go to school for a few days, and that was fine. I didn't want anyone's sympathy. I wasn't sure I would be able to live up to that kind of grief. I was too much in control of things, and that was neither good nor right; I should let go somehow.

I thought of Jolene, two rooms away from me, and tried to imagine what she looked like asleep. I stared into the dark space where I knew the open doorway was and tried to imagine that by staring I would come closer to her. I would send out a signal to draw her to me, or see something about her through the dark. It was all a matter of getting through the darkness, and I had plenty of time to make that happen. That was the thought that finally sent me off to sleep.

THE FIRST few days were a blur of hospital food and doctors, thinking about Jolene and trying to carry on a normal conversation with my mother. Jolene couldn't be there except to drop me off and pick me up in her red Pacer. She was in charge of coordinating some events between the Mark Twain house and the Hartford museum, where she worked, in commemoration of the bicentennial coming up next year. I'd never seen her in work clothes before I lived with her, and I remember thinking at first that she looked thinner and taller than I knew she was. I could tell she enjoyed dressing up, even if she was always making disgusted faces at herself in the mirror. When she tied her hair back you could see how thin and pretty her face was, and all the freckles on her forehead that were the same red-brown color as her hair.

The doctors had my mother very sedated. Her neck and leg were in traction. They were afraid if they didn't keep her peaceful she might hurt herself. One of them explained this to me. He was a pudgy man with a close dark beard and watery eyes who said he was a good friend of my mother's. He kept looking at his clipboard as if it would tell him all the things he needed to say when he explained it to me.

There were a few times I remember my mother being alert enough to grab my hands and whisper excitedly. She said she was putting everything together; she said it all joined up in the end, and there was a way to see through things that were painful. Love was very, very important in this. She said a lot of things were "very, very important": one I remember was that I shouldn't be so holed-up in myself, like my father. After carrying on this way for a while something would catch in her mind and she'd start talking about how much she hated certain things, people who had ruined her life for her. I remember being perfectly aware that I was tuning her out whenever this happened. I'd ring for a nurse to come put some more sedative in her IV so she could sleep again, then I'd sit by, waiting for the whole cycle to repeat. Everyone promised I was doing a lot of good and said I should keep coming back.

At night in bed I thought of Jolene. I stared into the dark where the door was and imagined her coming out of it. I thought of her doing this in many ways: sleep-walking with her arms out in front of her and her eyes half-shut; stealing in quietly, pretending to look for something she had left here, then seeing me and saying "Oh, you're up," and coming to sit on my bed; or just leaning there against the door with one bare foot moving on top of the other and returning my stare, not saying anything.

THE MORNING I decided not to visit my mother at the hospital anymore I was up early. I stood in front of the mirror with my shirt off and looked at myself. My arms were thin then and my shoulders had points on them like wing tips. I had grown almost as tall as I would ever be; still, I was shaped like a child in many ways. My hair was brown and so thick and wiry it stood out on the sides. I knew my features were too delicate to be considered really handsome, but I wasn't bad looking. I saw how girls looked at me and understood what it meant.

I wasn't sure how I would tell Jolene, but I knew as soon as I got out of bed that morning that I was finished visiting my mother at the hospital for a while. I put on a new T-shirt and jeans and yanked on the sleeves of the shirt so it would look worn. I was reading a book then called *Blind Date*, which I didn't like. I'd read *The Painted Bird*, and although it had scared me, I liked it a lot. That was when I used to read much more. Before I went to high school I read all the time—whenever there was nothing else to take up my attention. Most of the books I read were science fiction and fantasy—stories about men on different planets, having sex in outer space, sometimes with intelligent plants and robots, or Martians with extra limbs. My mother said my reading was an unhealthy habit. She said I was living in an imaginary world, but that didn't make me stop. When I began to realize how strange other people at high school thought I was—that was when I stopped reading so much.

It wasn't long before I heard Jolene getting up. "What time does the bus get here?" I asked her when she came into the kitchen to put some water on.

She yawned and pushed a fist at her mouth. Then she made her eyes wide and blinked a few times, like she was having trouble seeing. "What bus?" she asked.

"For school. I don't feel like walking."

"It's Saturday, Charlie."

"Saturday?"

"Mm-hmm." She gave me a serious look with her eyebrows squaring together. "No school on Saturday, remember?" She was smiling now.

"Boy, am I out of it."

"Well, it's to be expected." Her feet squeaked on the linoleum as she went back across the kitchen. The light was too dim for me to see anything through the nightgown she had on, which was just as well. I didn't like this feeling of spying on her. "I'll be out in a second," she said. "You want a shower?"

"No."

"Then I'll take my time and use up all the hot water." She stuck her tongue out at me and disappeared around the corner.

Jolene and my mother had met each other by dating the same man, when I was about seven years old. My mother had been seeing him for six months, Jolene a little longer than that. They didn't know about each other, though, until it was all over. His name was Don and he had told them both at different times that he wanted to marry them. That was just a ploy to make himself look more sincere than he was; he knew that neither of them would ever marry him and he was safe making his promises. Later, when Jolene and my mother started getting to know each other, they compared notes and that's when all this came out.

Don was smooth, but he was also crazy. He lived off

money from his father, who was a millionaire several times over, the only condition being that Don had to visit a psychiatric hospital of his father's choice twice a week for intensive treatment. He was always baldly honest about his problems when he talked to my mother. Sometimes when he was at our house he would announce things all of a sudden, like when and how often he took a shit in a day, or the fact that his parents used to walk around naked a lot while he was growing up. All of the things he said had to do with his analysis and what he told us he was "uncovering." There was never a question in my mind: he was crazy. Often I had the impression he actually enjoyed being crazy—that it satisfied some long-standing spite he had for the rational world.

But he drove a nice car, he dressed carefully, and in a strange way he treated my mother well. He was as insistent about buying her things and being affectionate as he was about confessing his problems. I think my mother needed this combination of demands he made, as a nurse and a lover, but I don't think she ever loved him. When he wasn't around, if I said his name or asked about him, she would smile and shake her head. "What a weirdo," she'd say, and keep smiling so I knew she liked him even though she was bewildered too.

Then one day Don showed up with Jolene on his arm. Jolene said later that she thought he was taking her to meet his mother. That's what he had told her. It was a strange afternoon. The four of us sat down together in the living room and Don had kind of a nervous break-down. Jolene and my mother were forced to give up their outrage so they could take care of him. He was weeping and shaking all over because of what he said he'd done to himself. My mother told me later that she and Jolene were just too startled by the whole thing to hate each other for the usual reasons. That's why they got to be best friends. Don moved to Florida and neither of them had anything more to do with him.

After that Jolene was at our house every weekend, and sometimes once or twice during the week as well. Satur-days she and my mother would do things together—shop, sit in the sun, play tennis, or just go out. I went with them sometimes, but not often. I knew I held them back and changed the ways they acted toward each other. Besides, most of the things they liked to do were boring. At night they would come back to my mother's and the three of us would eat dinner for about five hours while they got drunk. Often Jolene would stay over and spend most of Sunday morning with my mother as well, talking in the kitchen. I never paid much attention to what they said, but the feeling of what went on between them was comforting. There was a kind of soothing endlessness about it, though I was never sure who was soothing who.

Jolene looked like she'd been thinking about things when she came back into the room after her shower. She gave me a knowing kind of look, and said, "Come with me to work today?"

"What?" I said.

"Sure. I'm off at noon. We could do something."

"Do something like what?"

"There's an Impressionist exhibit I haven't gotten to look at yet. It isn't opening till next week, but I could get us in."

I nodded to give myself time to think. "That's nice of you," I said.

Her mouth stiffened a little. "Nothing formal, Charlie," she said. She tossed her hair away and went back into the kitchen to start her breakfast. "We'll have a good time. Then maybe we can swing by and see Mary."

"'Swing by.' Nobody swings by there." It was easier to be frank about this with her in the other room, not looking at me. "I'm not going back there for a few days. I'm sick of it."

"All right. But we can still have a good time."

"Sure," I said. "I'm sure we can."

As LONG as there were things to joke about we were comfortable with each other. Her boss's name was Mark Blow, pronounced "plow," and it was lucky for us he didn't ever work Saturdays. I had so many nicknames for him by the end of the day I couldn't have said his name out loud to anyone, certainly not him. She had to cut off one phone call because I had made her laugh so much. I was sitting across from her at Blow's desk when the person called. All I said was, "Have we got a job for you, Mr. Blow," very quietly.

She was able to control herself for a second, then she looked up at me sitting where he should have been, swallowed once to keep it down, and couldn't stop herself. "Hold," she whispered into the phone. When she'd calmed down she said, "You don't know how funny that is—you don't even know him. You have to stop." She glanced at her watch. "There's two hours left for me to finish looking at these things, and I don't want to have to stay any longer than that, so no jokes." She lifted the phone and pressed a button to get the caller back, keeping her eyes away from me, and leaned back in her chair. "This is Jolene Shore, how can I help? Oh God, I'd been waiting to hear about that!" she said. Her finger moved onto her forehead, seeming to touch and not touch her at the same time, just where the veins had stood out a moment before.

There were also moments we had nothing to joke about, like when we were looking at the Renoir paintings downstairs. Everything was set up as it should be, she said, except for some of the alarm wiring and most of the lighting, which was why they hadn't opened the exhibit yet. There were three dim, white rooms full of paintings and ladders.

One model Renoir used I thought looked a lot like Jolene, only heavier. I told her that, in general, I thought Renoir either loved fat women, or loved making all women look fat. She smiled nervously and didn't say which one she thought it was. "The word is 'voluptuous,' not 'fat,' Charlie. Nothing is fat in art," she said.

"Oh, well, la-de-da," I said.

The painting that reminded me most of Jolene was a woman with bare shoulders combing her hair in a round mirror.

"She's so innocent," Jolene said. I'd been there awhile looking at it, and hadn't even heard her come up behind me. "Don't you think?" she asked.

I didn't think she was innocent at all. I had the feeling she was made to look much younger and sweeter than she must have been in real life when Renoir did the painting. "No," I said, "she reminds me of you, actually. She's pretty nice."

There was a pause, like the narrow space under something that's just collapsed. "As soon as you say a thing like that, it isn't true, you know. You've forced it," she said. She took a step closer to me so I could feel her heat coming through the back of my shirt.

"Sorry," I said. "But it *was* true." I knew this was the wrong thing to say, and I also knew how oddly I had said it, almost as if I didn't believe myself.

"See, now you've created something that didn't have to

be there," she whispered. "Am I supposed to believe you? Am I supposed to do something? What do I do?"

"Jeez—take it easy. No wonder you and that guy Don had a field day in heaven—couple of neurotics." I was staring so hard at the painting I couldn't see its features anymore, only the individual brush strokes and dabs of paint.

"Let me tell you something, Charlie. It's very easy to end up with exactly the kind of relationship you don't want and the kind of thing that's worst for you. That's how it is. That's why I'm telling you, you don't force things like what you just said to me, you leave them alone."

"Slow down," I said.

"What?" she said.

We looked at each other and I couldn't tell what was making her so upset, though I was pretty sure it wasn't just what I'd said to her. It couldn't have been, because it went beyond insulting her. Then, looking at her I couldn't help thinking about how much I really did like her—everything about her—the way she stood, the thin shape of her face, the skin just under her eyes that pulled and wrinkled, expressing things she didn't even know she was expressing. I wasn't trying to make any of my thoughts show in my face, but they must have just the same. She smiled and put a half-curled hand up against my cheek. "You're a dear," she said. "You really are."

I didn't say anything. I let her push her hand back

through my hair and take hold of my neck like it was something she wished she could own.

"There's more to see," she said.

I followed her eyes around the room. "A lot," I said.

"Cézanne," she said. She let go of my neck and looked back at the painting of the woman brushing her hair. "I appreciate what you said, Charlie. I really do. It's sweet." Then, coldly, "Don't get me wrong."

"Oh, not at all," I said, and moved a few steps away. I didn't want her to see how much I was smiling to myself, trying to imagine what all that coldness was supposed to hide.

On Monday I went back to school.

My English teacher said if I wrote a paper about that book *Blind Date,* he would forget all the work I had to make up. My other teachers were not quite as easy. I had theorems to memorize for geometry, a biology lab to get through alone, and two dynasties of Chinese history to read about. I didn't mind the work. I thought it was a relief to be so distracted.

Most of the kids at school didn't know who I was or why I'd been gone—it was the teachers I worried about. They'd all been told about my mother. But I hoped that as long as I acted busy they would leave me alone. They'd shake their heads and say to each other, "Well, he's coping. He'll be fine." I didn't want them suggesting things, like a visit to the school psychiatrist, or a session with one of them after class, unloading my feelings.

This is what I came up with as a thesis sentence for my paper on *Blind Date*: "The cool tone of this book mirrors the protagonist's own indifferent façade." I thought it explained many things about the book that had both pleased and frustrated me. When my paper was finished I wanted someone to read it, so I asked Jolene. She'd had a lot of wine with dinner. We were in the living room and she was still drinking while I entertained her with stories about things that had happened in school that week. It was Friday night and I think she was happy not to be alone—celebrating by getting a little drunk.

"I'd love to see your paper," she said. "You clean up." She pointed into the kitchen at the dishes in the sink. "Do a good job and I'll just sit right here and read your paper." She poured what was left of the wine into her glass and then held the empty bottle out at me to throw away. "So, go get me your paper, Mr. Charlie-Genius."

The tone of her voice when she said that surprised me. I wasn't sure what she meant by it, whether it was a joke or a real challenge. I stood up. "You only have to proof-read. You don't even have to *try* to understand anything, if that's what you're worried about—though I can see there's little danger of comprehension in your condition." The paper was on the end table next to the couch, written on narrow-rule paper and folded in half. I picked it up and waved it in her face like a wand, then I dropped it on her. "Remember, you go left to right, from the top of the page. That's all you need to know," I said, and went to the kitchen.

"Left to right," she repeated. "Thanks."

There were a lot of dishes—the ice cream maker, a big pot with pasta stuck on the bottom of it, burned chicken and sesame seeds in the bottom of the frying pan, a saucepan with white sauce gummed up and hardened on the sides, salad bowls, plates, glasses, and breakfast stuff from the morning. I separated everything into piles according to size and filled the sink with soap and water. When I scrubbed, bits of burned food and soap went everywhere. I watched my reflection in the black window over the sink and was disappointed. The smile on my face was too orange and fierce. It didn't look like it understood anything about itself. My whole face seemed ugly and too thin to me, the way it flickered and bent in the glass like flames. "Kid," I mouthed at myself. I leaned in closer until I saw through my reflection into the night outside where a man was walking across the street with his dog, and two cold puffs of condensation formed on the glass under my nose. I leaned back. "Stupid goddamn kid," I said and watched my mouth open and close in the glass. I didn't even know whether or not I meant what I said.

Jolene was laughing madly about something in the living room and calling for me. I was pretty sure what she was laughing at would have to do with the section I had written about the main character, when he lives for two chapters with twin blond sisters and alternates his nights between their beds. I had used part of this as an example to define something about the author's deficient morals. I went and stood in front of Jolene with my arms sleeved in soapy water. "What?" I asked.

"Sit down," she said. She cleared a space for me on the couch and patted it with her hand. I sat. "Now look," she said. She had my paper open and was pointing at something.

"Give me that," I said, and snatched it away. A drop of water went across the page and turned blue, taking the ink with it. "Oh, shit," I said, and switched hands, but that only made matters worse: water was everywhere and words were running in streaks off the page. She grabbed it away and I grabbed it back. Then I held it up over my head, so she had to come around on top of me to get at it. I let it fall on the floor behind us and circled my arms around her waist. I held on to keep her from going over the back of the couch. Her chin was on my forehead and she was laughing, not resisting how close we were. I could feel the soap and water go through the back of her shirt and turn cold. "Ha-ha," I said, because I didn't know what else to say in this situation. I had won the game, but the game was finally too transparent to mean anything. I wasn't sure what should come next, but I had some ideas.

When she stopped laughing, and I could be fairly sure she had sensed the same things I had, I leaned forward and touched her Adam's apple with my lips. This was as easy to do as not to do. I kissed her tentatively at first, and when she didn't resist I opened my mouth to taste her and feel her pulse on my tongue. She was salty and smelled like powder. After a few seconds her weight changed, softened and settled against me, and her hands began moving down my arms, her fingers squeezing through my fingers. When she kissed me she went over everything on my face with her lips and tongue. I'd never known how the nerves in my face were connected with other nerves all over my back that would suddenly fire and release according to where she touched me.

"Are we being intimate, Charlie?" she asked. Strands of her hair were caught in mine, hanging between us. For an answer I slid my hands up under the back of her shirt and unhooked her bra. She pinned my wrists under her arms and shook her head. "I'm not some easy high school sweetie for you to take through the high school moves. Now, you relax." She released my hands. "Don't do things just because you *think* you know the right way to do them. That's when you don't."

We wound up on the floor, me leaning back against the couch and her between my legs leaning back against me. I teased her with my with fingertips all over her bare stomach and ribs and breasts. Then she pulled my hand down between her legs, guiding my fingers under hers. What she did sent jolts through her. It made her lean back harder and harder on me, her legs wrapping around mine. Then she let go of my finger and whispered, "Slow as you can." I could see the heartbeats burst and fade in her neck, and a splash of red growing on her chest like a rash. Then something was happening inside her—a kind of seizure or transformation. I'd never seen anything like it.

When it was over she rolled onto her side and closed her legs around my hand. "You're beautiful," I said. "That was amazing."

"You better believe it," she said, and inched her way up my chest with kisses until I was pinned under her. Then she stopped and seemed to be listening for something.

"What is it?" I asked.

"You're shaking."

"No," I said, "no, I'm not," and tried to smile. I was holding on to one of the legs on the table next to the couch, feeling the beveled wood in my palm, and trying to think of anything but what was about to happen.

"Are you cold?" she asked.

"No."

She pried my hand away and forced her fingers through mine like she had done before. Her arms were out straight against mine so that I could barely move and we had to synchronize our breathing. Then I knew how it would be. All my muscles released. I took a big breath and held it down as long as I could, felt our hands squeezing harder and harder together, heard things rattling on the table over us, heard her gasping, and that was the end of it.

We lay together until we were both asleep, and when I woke up she was next to me on her back, also awake, though I couldn't remember ever having separated. I was surprised, when I looked at her, not to feel at all ashamed or embarrassed by what I saw. The hair between her legs was thick and startlingly dark, almost brown, and there were thin wrinkles, like violin strings, on her hips and under her arms. I was also surprised that the parts of her that pleased me most to look at were not those parts that had always been hidden. It was parts of her like her neck and chest, which I had seen all along, that satisfied me for reasons I couldn't understand.

"How many girls have you done that with?" she wanted to know. She poked me in the shoulder. "Count them all, huh?"

I didn't answer. I had no idea whether to tell the truth or not—which would bother her more—and lay back on one arm to give myself a moment to think.

"Everyone in your class?" she asked.

"As a matter of fact, no. Just you."

She propped herself over me now. "Charlie," she said. She pushed me over onto my back. "You really mean it. I wish you'd said something." At first I thought she was only searching my face for a lie. Then I realized she wasn't searching, she was seeing something, and it was all the emotion and concern that came with seeing it that made her eyes so desperate. "Charlie," she kept saying, "Charlie."

"What?"

"You!" she said. "What the hell are we doing?" She turned away and looked like she might be about to get up.

I put my hand on her hip. "We're not forcing anything, remember?"

IN THE opening chapter of *Blind Date* the main character blows up a ski tram in Switzerland in order to kill one man. He is under contract to do this, and once he has finished, he skis down the mountain to sip espresso before phoning the man who hired him (for a million dollars) to do it—to tell him the job has been safely carried out. I had always wished for something like this in my life— not the violence but the extraordinary secret purpose of that man standing alone on the closed trail just before he does his work. He listens to the birds, checks his watch, and waits until he sees the tram in the distance ascending from the valley. Then he fuses the electronic detonation devices in his pack and watches the tram rip silently open, a noiseless black and red explosion with pieces of flaming metal and plastic falling softly to the snow. He watches just long enough to know his job is done, then he skis away through the woods.

I was like any other boy my age having this wish,

except I thought I had pretty much achieved it by sleeping with Jolene. We made love all that week, every chance we had. Sometimes when I was at school I would suddenly smell her through my clothes and feel my blood jump, or taste her when I bit my fingernails. I couldn't get away from it. I liked to look over the people in my class and imagine that I'd pretty much gone beyond anything they understood. I was as extraordinary and alone and full of secret purpose as that man on skis. It was harder to feel this way when I was with her.

I DIDN'T visit my mother until Wednesday that week. Her neck was out of traction, but not her leg, and she was in worse spirits than I had seen her since she got there. One of the nurses had explained to me that they were going to move her to another ward for counseling and therapy soon, and she was anxious about that. After the move it would only be a few more weeks before she could go home—depending on her leg and how she responded to crisis treatment, the nurse said.

I had already decided that I wouldn't wait for my mother to ask any questions about Jolene, I would speak first. I needed to have as much control of the situation as possible. So, when she had finished telling me what she knew about counseling and therapy and why she didn't expect it to help, I said, "Well, you'll be happy to know that Jolene and I have been getting along really, really well. That's *one* thing you don't need to worry about."

She closed her eyes for a second and let out a breath so it seemed like she was sinking back into the bed. She'd had her hair cut very short to make it easier for the nurses to wash. She called it her crazy-lady bowl cut, which I thought was appropriate, because it was so jagged and short. It also showed how much more white than brown her hair was becoming. "Just please remember what a favor she's doing for you," she said.

"Oh," I said, "I wouldn't ever forget that. But we really get along great. I don't think she minds me being there at all."

My mother gave me a look like I ought to know she wouldn't take that seriously. She might appreciate my efforts to put her at ease by covering things up, but we should both know the truth. "You'll never really know, will you, either of you, how badly I feel for putting you through this."

I shrugged. "That isn't really the issue," I said.

"It is, and I want you to know it. I *do* know how hard it's been. And if there's one thing that makes me want to stay alive long enough to get out of this"—she looked around her like she couldn't quite find the words to describe it—"damn hospital, it's so that things can be back to normal for you two."

"Mom, listen, would it help if I told you—Jolene and I are actually both kind of enjoying it, the change of pace?"

"What are you talking about?"

"I'm just trying to make you see this so you can feel better about it . . ." I took a breath and looked at my hands. "Really, you don't need to worry about me. I'm fine. I'm more fine than ever. Jolene and I really *like* being together." I smirked a little at that and felt myself blushing.

"Are you saying what I think you're saying?"

"What do you think I'm saying?"

"Don't be cute with me, Charlie—and look at me when I'm talking to you. Jesus Christ," she said. She pulled herself up on her elbows so that her leg swung slightly in its sling. There were two long pins going through her just above the knee, which I hated to look at. "Look at me," she said again.

"What?" I said, and met eyes with her, still smirking.

"I should have known."

"Known what?"

"Just like your goddamn father."

"What's that supposed to mean?"

"Just get out of here."

"What, did he sleep with your best friend too?"

"Sleep with her?" Her eyes were jumping out at me. "You want me to believe you're actually sleeping with that woman—twice your age? That's sick. That's a sick thing to try to put over on me." She lay back, apparently convinced now that the whole thing was only a sham. "You don't have to go that far to hurt me."

"Nobody's trying to hurt you."

"Oh, of course not." She rolled her eyes. "Whatever put such a silly idea in my head?" She smiled bitterly, as though she'd finally come to understand a conspiracy against her, and she could feel glad but she could also feel sorry for herself about it. "You know, if you really want to hurt a person there are better ways. But you *can't* really expect me to believe you're sleeping with a woman—a frigid woman, for years now, believe me, I know about it . . ." She shook her head and didn't say anything for a moment. "There are better ways to hurt someone."

"What are you talking about?"

"You know perfectly well. Just leave me alone." She closed her eyes. "Leave your old mother alone." I saw her hands had locked together so hard it was white under her fingernails and all her veins and bones showed. I never tried to tell her the truth about anything again after that.

I BEGAN to know Jolene, and in some ways I liked her more, some ways less. I noticed all of her mannerisms: the way she picked at her fingers when I talked to her, or the way she kept her head tilted slightly to one side when she walked, like she was enjoying some distant sight or fragrance. There were other times she would stand still with a kind of wistful, all-knowing look on her face. I had always considered those moments as a part of some great mystery that was connected with her beauty. Now I saw it was only a pose, and what made her stand still like that was just the ordinary kind of indecision or forgetfulness that makes any person stop and wonder what the next thing is they're supposed to do. In general, I saw Jolene liked to seem much more spontaneous and carefree than she really was, and she used all her mannerisms to that end. Sometimes I could hardly see her anymore. Sometimes she was just a collection of gestures and flounces and stances and stock phrases that always came at the same time, and I couldn't even be sure she was a living person at all.

That was on the surface. But under the surface I began to see we were very much alike. We responded to things the same way. We could burst out laughing together, without either of us having said what was so funny. We even woke up together most mornings, alarm or no alarm, as if our eyes were synchronized. I used to wonder whether we were actually alike to start with, or if it was just living together that made us alike; I thought about that a good deal, but I'm not sure it matters at all.

I remember Saturday, a week after that first night we spent together. We were at the school play, standing in the front foyer during intermission and looking around at all the people, not saying much to each other, when I began to have a feeling I didn't recognize. It was a cold, locked feeling, like something had suddenly grabbed me inside and wouldn't let go. I tried not to think about it, but my legs were sweating. Somehow I knew this was a psychological thing—a new trick my mind was playing—and I would be fine again in a few seconds. I still had my balance and I could see perfectly well what was going on around me. There were parents and kids everywhere. A man in a blue jacket was standing close, his back to me, speaking in a loud voice with two or three other parents. The air smelled sweet from cookies, pineapple punch, and people's breath. I tried to see across the room to the exit and wondered how I would ever get there if I had to.

Jolene leaned across and whispered in my ear some trite phrase about how crowds are the loneliest places. Then she said, "No, truth is I just can't stop thinking about what we were doing right before we came here. I keep looking at people and thinking they know all about it. It's stupid. That's what I keep thinking." She blushed and kicked one of her feet up against the wall behind her.

"Same here," I said.

"And frankly I'd much rather still be at home," she said.

I watched her tongue go across her lips. "Exactly," I said. "But we can't do that forever."

"Which is why we're standing here like a couple of morons."

"Wallflowers," I said and took a step away from her to stand with my feet wide, letting the air cool my legs.

She tilted her head at me, as if this was a new and interesting thing to have said. "Is that what you are at school, Charlie—a wallflower?"

"No, I don't think so. I have some friends."

"Man, was I trouble when I was your age." She rolled her eyes. "Nobody understood, let alone me." She pressed two fingers to her throat, like I might have forgotten who she meant when she said "me." The bracelets made a sound on her wrist, then slipped down her arm. "I was just trying to find myself, I guess—doing a lot of stupid things in the process. *That* was the problem. Ever heard of 'free love'?"

I shook my head.

"Well, these things can confuse you—they're meant to be confusing, I think. Wasn't till a few years ago that I started making any sense out of anything. Just about the time I met your mother." She blinked and let her eyes stay closed for a second. "Yeah, about then. She can be a really smart, smart woman, you know, despite everything."

I nodded. "That's more than a few years, though," I said.

"So it is." She let her foot slide off the wall and started picking at one of her fingers. "We won't mention it."

"Okay. Tell me about free love." The lights blinked on and off twice. People started moving for the doors, talking faster and drinking the last of their punch.

"It's not something you explain, it's something you try to do—only the truth is it's a bunch of made-up garbage, if you want to know. No," she corrected herself, pulling her hair over one shoulder and thinking, "the thing about demystifying sex, and love—taking it for what it is—that isn't bullshit. It's what people do with the idea. Never mind." She slipped her hand under my arm and led us back to our seats, where it was cooler and I could feel the sweat drying. I thought we should sit like all the other people around us, watching as students I didn't know pretended to be people they weren't up on a stage. But we left about fifteen minutes into the act, after Jolene whispered in my ear that this was boring.

Later that night she asked me what it was I thought she liked most about me. I said maybe my sense of humor, or my personality. She said no, she liked me because I hadn't become what I was going to be for the rest of my life yet. She said this made me diaphanous. When I asked her to explain, she said, "Do you ever get the feeling when we're making love that you can't tell the two of us apart? Like, who's who?" I told her I thought I did, though I was less sure about it than I let on. She said, "That's because you're diaphanous, which is what I like." I was glad she didn't ask what I liked most about her. I didn't know how I would have answered.

THAT BREATHLESS, locked-up feeling continued to bother me. Sometimes at night, lying in bed and listening to Jolene sleep, thinking about things that had happened during the day, it would happen. My legs would start to sweat. Then I'd press the palms of my hands against the cool wall behind us and think, *Cool, cool, easy,* and similar things to make peaceful ideas go through me, so I would relax. Her bed was deep, soft, and comfortable. I tried to think about that. It was so big I could lie diagonally on my stomach with my arms out and no part of us but our feet would touch. She said I was an unfriendly sleeper and sometimes I fought her away in my dreams. I don't know about that.

I do know about the nights I lay there looking at the square of light from the window shining on the wall next to us, and a faint shadow of the curtains moving there, while I tried to make myself feel cool and easy. I could never free my mind long enough to see what was really bothering me. Some nights I was awake and thinking until nothing made sense anymore, even day-to-day things. People's faces or voices, things they had said to me, these would circle one another in my brain until I couldn't say what was real and what wasn't. Then I was half-asleep for most of the next day and nothing seemed real then either.

I began to explore Jolene's apartment building during the few hours I had to myself after school. On days I didn't ride the bus out to the hospital I would come home, make a sandwich, and take it with my homework to find a quiet place somewhere in the unused parts of the building. Jolene explained to me that these apartments were never finished because the original owner had lost his backing. The new owner wanted to wait until the recession passed before he spent any more money. I knew how to get into these parts of the building from the ground floor and liked to stay up there until the light was gone. There were big windows in the halls, and dust, nails, and sawdust covering the floors.

After a few days I discovered an unlocked apartment on the fifth floor. Like all the apartments on that floor, this one would have been a luxury unit. It had an open, spacious feeling with windows going almost to the floor. There were pipes coming out of the walls where plumbing would be, and AC boxes hanging by their cables where the sheetrock hadn't been finished. I liked to sit here looking east and watching the sun turn red on the trees below me, or yellow in the last fall heat and haze— so bright yellow, sometimes, that the dirt and sawdust would begin to sparkle on the floor.

Jolene knew where I went. When I told her about it, she said she didn't see any harm. She thought if the super wasn't smart enough to have the place locked up, it was just as well for someone like me to be up there keeping an eye on things. Sometimes she would come to find me, if it was starting to get dark or she was worried I had fallen asleep and didn't know what time it was.

Then we would sit together and imagine this was our apartment. The darker it got the easier it was to imagine how it would be, where the walls would separate rooms, and what furniture we would put where. Then we'd race each other back down the dark halls to her apartment.

JOLENE FOUND out before I did that my mother was coming home from the hospital. She'd gone to visit her after work while I studied for a test at home. I was on her bed, trying to solve some practice proofs from a test the teacher had given the year before.

"Let's go up and see the sunset," she said when she found me there in the bedroom.

"One minute," I said. I thought I'd almost gotten something figured out about the complementary angles of a parallelogram.

"We don't have a minute, Charlie."

I looked up at her. Her eyes were swollen and seemed smaller. "What happened?" I asked.

"I'll tell you. Let's go upstairs."

We went to the empty apartment and stood in the middle of what we liked to think of as the living room, between two west-facing windows. The light was fierce, streaming through the dirt we'd stirred up around us. Jolene hugged herself and drew patterns on the floor with the tip of her shoe. The sun had gone under a thin layer of clouds and was lighting them up. Then I watched as it slipped out below and the colors in the window pane began to glare and flash, disappearing in a glaze.

"She's coming home this weekend," Jolene said.

"I figured that's what it was," I said. Then it dawned on me. "You mean this weekend, as in three days from now?"

She nodded. "Saturday or Sunday. She's pretty set on it." She cleared her throat. "I mean, we couldn't go on like this anyway, right?" She moved her foot more vigorously across the floor to erase the patterns she'd drawn, then stopped and looked at me.

"I don't know if we could or not."

"Oh, come on. Don't be stupid."

"I don't know," I said. "Maybe there's a way." I didn't mean for my voice to sound as small or full of hope as it did. "We'll have to think about it." I watched the sun stretch out and begin to disappear over the land. "There must be something," I said.

She didn't answer and we were quiet awhile.

"It's so nice up here," she said. "Let's just live here."

"We might run into a few problems with that," I said.

I heard her move closer behind me, then I felt her breath in my ear. She hugged me, moving slightly up and down on her toes, and slid a hand inside my shirt. I saw one shoe, then the other, come sailing out from behind me. "Let's stay up here tonight," she said. "We can bring candles and blankets and just stay awake all night together." When she said that I felt the sweat jump and break out down my legs, and I had to breathe hard to make it stop. "What is it?" she asked, letting go of me a little. "What's wrong?"

I faced her, pushed her arms away, and tried to think of something to say. "I don't know," I said.

She was searching my face the way she had the first night we made love. Only this time I saw she was looking back at me in exactly the same way I was looking at her—with the same kinds of searching and complying things in her face. And seeing that I began to understand myself. I understood what I had always wanted from her, what I wanted to show her about myself, and understood there weren't going to be words for it. "Let me," I said, and spread my shirt on the floor for her. "Just be still," I said. And all the time I made love to her some part of my mind was perfectly aware that people all over the world were making the same minutes pass in ways that didn't matter. I told myself that was all right, but I still felt the indifference everywhere around me. I was alone and the dirt and sawdust were digging at my hands. She squeezed her legs around my sides to make me go slower, even tried to hold me down, I thought, but I wouldn't be held. I lunged at her like an animal. When I collapsed I knew I had shown her nothing of what I had intended—nothing I felt.

She moved under me. "I wasn't really ready for that, you know," she said.

"I know."

She pushed hard at my shoulder with the heel of her hand to make me get off her, then before I could respond she pulled me down again, just as hard, and whispered, "It's all right. It's all right," and kept whispering that, smoothing her hands over my back. We went downstairs a while later and never returned to that part of the building together again.

The next few days we spent almost as much time at my mother's house as we did at Jolene's, trying to clean up and make the place feel "lived in" again, as Jolene said. Jolene liked my mother's shower better than hers because it got such good pressure and because there was an overhead heat lamp that turned everything red and warm when it was on, like the inside of an eyelid. It was hard to tell, sometimes, with that lamp on and the water going, whether we were asleep or awake—whether our eyes were open or half-closed. I'd never paid attention to this before, and had rarely used my mother's bathroom in the past. When I told Jolene that she didn't seem to have heard. Whenever my mother came up in conversation those last days Jolene and I spent together, neither of us acted like we believed anything we were saying. It was like we couldn't quite comprehend her or the fact that she would be returning.

The last night we brought all my stuff home and ended up sleeping there on the fold-out bed in the living room.

Then in the morning I stayed to clean up some more while Jolene went to the hospital. I was in my mother's bedroom, dusting one last time, when I heard Jolene's car pull in the driveway. They were out there awhile, and when I still didn't hear a car door open or close, I went to the living room window to have a look. It was hard to see through the glare on Jolene's windshield and the reflection of our house in it. I couldn't be sure of what I was seeing at first, then I saw they were leaning out of their seats and they had their arms around each other. My mother's arm was lying across Jolene's back and she was sobbing while Jolene looked straight out the side window at nothing. When they separated my mother was smiling and wiping at her eyes. Then she took Jolene's face in her hands while she said something, and Jolene put her hands on top of my mother's.

I looked away. I was shivering. I didn't want any part of this—whatever they had to say to each other. Then I took a deep breath and felt my blood release, realizing, finally, that whatever was said and whoever said it, now was too late to worry about how life had changed for us.

I heard a door shut and saw them coming up the front steps with their arms around each other, my mother's leg in a cast out in front of them. Both of them were laughing at the effort this took. When I threw open the door I looked straight at Jolene. She winked at the same time I did, then stuck her tongue out at me a little, and I knew everything would be all right. "Welcome home," I said in a loud voice, and stood aside to let them pass. Later that night Jolene came into my room. I wasn't sleeping anyway. We were dead quiet, barely breathing.

MY MOTHER and I never really talked about the fall I lived with Jolene. Sometimes I thought about the one time in the hospital when I had tried to tell her the truth, and wondered if she ever went back over our exchange—if she might not suspect her own instant rejection of what I'd said and start looking for another sign. If she did, I never knew about it. One thing I learned about my mother in everything that had happened: once she saw something one way she'd never see it as anything else. She did this without knowing, I think, in order to shut out whatever she didn't understand or want to face.

Jolene and my mother remained friends, though they saw much less of each other and nothing was the same as it had been. My mother explained to me once that she thought this was because she had betrayed Jolene. She said she had betrayed Jolene in the same way she had betrayed everyone who knew her—by proving that the only person she would ever really care about in the world was herself. She said knowing this wasn't easy for people to live with; it was the last thing a friend wanted to know about you. I tried to assure her that no one actually thought badly of her; people were more understanding than she knew. But that wasn't the way she ever thought of it.

That winter and spring I skipped school often to meet with Jolene, and spent many weekends out of town, at friends' houses which didn't really exist. For an afternoon and a night, or sometimes just a night, Jolene and I would pretend that time had doubled over on itself. We would imagine that we were as close as we ever had been, and as close as we used to imagine we always would be. But it became more and more difficult to pretend—not because we didn't still love each other. We did. And we couldn't ever keep from blaming each other for this, or for the way the situation wasn't what we wished it would be.

That spring Jolene and I went to Lake Erie, where she'd spent her summers as a kid. We ended up in a little Ohio town just south of Sandusky Bay. I told my mother I would be camping with a made-up friend at a made-up campground in Old Saybrook, and that I wouldn't be back until Tuesday, which she thought was fine. She liked the fact that I suddenly seemed to have such a busy social life, and liked to tell me sometimes that good friends were more important than anything else in life. Jolene had a week's vacation; she told my mother, and anyone else who knew her, she was going to spend it in Denver with the brother she hadn't seen in years. This was the kind of clean break from reality Jolene and I had wished for all winter—four full days with no fear of the phone ringing, people stopping by, or anyone seeing us in town.

The place we stayed at was called the Huntsman's Inn. Our room had low ceilings, green carpeting, and thick acrylic drapes. The walls were shiny wood paneling that soaked up the light and returned it a blond varnish color. We'd driven all day and when we arrived we fell right into the middle of the bed. We undressed and explored each other in the ways we always did at first—to see that everything we remembered about each other was still the same. Her skin was cool and heavy. There was the same mole on her prickly shin, the same smell in her hair, same heat in her neck and cold in her instep. We moved slowly, both of us knowing in a detached way that we would probably enjoy this one time more than any other time all weekend, and fell asleep with the lights on and the TV flickering, head to foot in the middle of the bed. Much later she must have gotten up, darkened the room, and locked the door, because that's how it was when I woke up.

"Charlie," she was saying. "Charlie, are you awake?" I wanted to see if I could tell something about whatever was bothering her before I got involved in it, so I didn't answer. I kept my eyes shut and waited. She flipped restively onto her back and kicked her leg once. I heard the mattress springs resound under us. "I wish he'd wake up," she said, and then lay still so long I thought she must have gone back to sleep. Finally she sat up. "Charlie," she said. She was shaking my leg now. "Look, wake up," she said, still shaking my leg, "I need to talk to you." I grunted and sniffed sharply to make it seem as if she had surprised me. She came around next to me and leaned down so that her hair fell across my face. "We've got to talk," she said more quietly.

"Talk about what?" I asked, still trying to sound like someone coming out of a deep sleep. I pulled her against me and pressed my fingers into the soft muscles between her shoulder blades. "Tell me," I said.

"Just—just stay with me and don't go back to sleep yet." She didn't say anything while I continued to rub her back. Then she gave me a little push and said, "I honestly cannot stand the thought of you with anyone else. You know that? I can't *stand* it." She paused. "There—I said it; you can hate me if you want, but at least I said it."

"Whoa—slow down. I don't hate you," I said.

She took a deep breath and I felt her weight increase against me. "All right," she said. "You're right."

"First of all, I couldn't stand it any better than you could. You know that. Secondly, this age thing—you're not that much older than me, if that's what's making you worry. Twelve years isn't that big a deal. And thirdly . . ."

"Oh, Charlie, yes it is; twelve years is a very big deal at this point in your life."

"Thirdly, you and I can do anything we want. We don't have to do something just because it looks like the 'right' thing to do. I don't *have* to follow some program for the adolescent boy . . ."

"It isn't a program, it's just knowing what's normal and what's got to happen. There are some facts in the world." She rolled away so her back was toward me and didn't say anything for a while, then she rolled toward me again and put her hand on my face. "Tell me, Charlie—if we can do anything, then why don't we just keep driving and never go back? You know? I mean, we're this far, why don't we keep going?"

"Because," I said, "we couldn't. That just isn't the real world."

"Exactly. That's exactly what I'm trying to say." She was quiet again. Then she said, "Let's just live with this for the next three days, okay? Let's just think about it and live with it and try to come to some kind of decision. Maybe if we can meet up again ten years from now, if we haven't killed ourselves from being so goddamn bored and lonely in the process, then fine—we can take up where we left off."

"What are you saying?"

"You know what I'm saying."

I tried to separate myself from the situation long enough to believe that what she had said was the final truth—tried to make it sink in and have an effect, but I couldn't. We'd talked this way before, and it never really meant anything to me. I couldn't ever make it real enough to comprehend.

"What if I was some old bald fart with glasses," I asked. "That would fix everything for you, wouldn't it? Some old schoolteacher, or something, with a cane and a little mustache." I laughed, trying to picture it, and felt the bed shake. Soon she was laughing too.

"The only thing it would fix for sure is my sex drive," she said.

"Oh, that's right. I almost forgot; grown men don't turn you on."

She flipped onto her stomach and didn't say anything. I could see I'd hit something without meaning to—something that went beyond what I'd said, and made her wonder about herself in a way she didn't want to. I remembered what my mother had said once about Jolene being frigid for years, and though I was sure this was an exaggeration, I also thought some part of it might explain her attraction to me. We never talked much about that—why or how she was attracted to someone my age. I don't think either of us wanted to acknowledge the strangeness in it.

"You know what?" I asked to distract her. She kicked up one of her feet behind her. "This may sound crazy, but what I like best about this, when we're together, what I like best is that there's no one here but us. You know what I mean? Do you ever get that feeling? No one but us."

"Not recently," she said. She turned onto her back and stared at the ceiling. Outside a car swung into a parking space and for a second the light cut through the blinds and went across Jolene's face. Her eyes were bright yellow, the color of new leaves, with almost no pupils in the sudden light. Then she was in the shadows again. "Charlie, do you think there's something wrong with me?" she asked.

"Wrong?"

She nodded, still staring at the ceiling. "My taste," she said seriously, then laughed, apparently taken aback by her own seriousness.

"I'll check," I said, and kissed her—probed the smooth fronts of her teeth as if I were looking for something. "Nope. Nothing wrong there. How about . . ." I waited, letting her guess where my next move would be. "Here," I said, and tried to double over fast to get my tongue in her navel.

She sat up and batted me away, laughing, then pulled me back down. "You really think I'll just let you do anything you want, don't you?" she asked. "That's what you really like, isn't it."

"Ah-ha," I said. "Not completely, but there's certainly something to it."

"Sure. You can't fool me."

Soon we'd forgotten all the things we were talking about.

There was something new between us that weekend,

though, some kind of reserve or awareness that came from all the talk about things ending. We spent a lot of time worrying about people who would come into our separate futures, imagining them as if they were there with us and we had to perform for them. Jolene was always at a distance, I thought, proving herself to me in someone else's eyes. As much as I could, I tried not to fall into this with her, but it wasn't easy. She was too compelling, the way she hung on me and asked me to describe everything I knew about myself and her, as if she hadn't already heard it before.

It was cold and overcast most of the weekend. We stayed in her car when we were out, and only went on a few short walks near the closed-down amusement park at the end of the beach. She showed me where she'd hung out with her friends around the bay; where she'd gotten drunk for the first time and jumped off a bridge on a dare; the beach where she'd lost her virginity. Sometimes I had the feeling she really was presenting me with her whole life, and asking me please, please to say it was good enough for something—I didn't know what—at the same time fully expecting my rejection.

On the long drive home she made up a game where we would imagine we were seeing each other again for the first time in ten years. She always set the scenario.

"You walk into a little restaurant in Boston and I'm sitting there waiting for my coffee. You see me first because

I'm looking out the window and I don't see you at all. What do you do?" she asked.

I sighed, crossed my leg up over my knee, and didn't say anything.

"Oh—you see I have a wedding ring on my finger, but I'm all alone, and you think I look great. My hair's shorter." She patted her hair and looked straight ahead at the road. "What do you do?"

"I'd probably say, Come on back to my place or something, I don't know—'One last time, for old time's sake' maybe."

"Oh, come on, you would not. You're too shocked to say something like that."

"Probably. I'm not really into this."

She acted like she hadn't heard me. "One more, then it's really your turn. Say I'm at the beach in Rhode Island, and I've got two kids with me you think might be mine, but you aren't sure. You're lying there by yourself and you look up and there I am, blocking the sun, covered with freckles, with these two kids."

"One-piece or a bikini?" I asked.

"What?" She had to think a second to catch my drift. "God, is that all you ever think of? Sex?"

"It is if we're going to play this stupid game. If I *could* tell you half of what I really think then I wouldn't have any problem. Don't you get it?"

We looked across the empty seat at each other. "I do

get it," she said. "I'm really sorry. I was just trying to have fun. I didn't mean to trivialize anything for you." She caught my hand for a second, then let it drop.

"You aren't 'trivializing' anything. It's just a dumb game," I said, but neither of us believed anything we had to say anymore.

We rode a long way in silence and every time we passed an exit for one of the big freeways north or south with signs to Columbus, Pittsburgh, or Philadelphia, both of us would look up quickly, thinking the same thing—wondering how hard it would be to make that turn off and keep driving, imagining how we might cheer each other on if we did.

But we followed signs for New York and points east. We stopped to eat, and kept driving in silence. Even though those four days together had been a strain—all the acting like doomed lovers, like this was our last and only time together and we had to do all the appropriate things to ignore and acknowledge our inevitable parting—I realized, in spite of this, and despite everything seeming so illusory, that whatever had happened was still completely between us. We would both remember it tomorrow. We would even miss it. Certainly we would miss it, even if it hadn't been the best time we'd ever had together. Thinking about this I began to see that what had always been between us was the biggest illusion of all. It was a world we had agreed on, apart from anything else in the world.

It was real, but it would vanish the moment we turned away, when all the differences between us and the ways we saw things ceased to matter. Maybe something would remain for a while in the ways we thought about each other, but even that was bound not to last.

We lay like mummies that night in Jolene's bed, waiting for morning, and never touched. She drove me to school and then brought my stuff home to my mother's. Jolene knew my mother would be at work. I don't think we even said good-bye formally, just patted each other's hands, kissed once, and said something about another weekend soon.

A few weeks went by and neither my mother nor I heard anything from Jolene. I wasn't surprised by this, but I hadn't entirely expected it, either. I thought of calling her once or twice myself, but couldn't quite see why I should. Then one night my mother decided we ought to drive by and see what had become of her. I wasn't doing anything—school had just gotten out and I was waiting to start my summer job lifeguarding at the outdoor YMCA pool. I told my mother maybe it would be a good idea for us to call Jolene before we barged in on her. She agreed this was the right thing to do and went to the phone.

"That's funny," she said after a few seconds. She pressed down the receiver and dialed again.

"What?" I asked.

"Her phone's been disconnected. I wonder—she wouldn't go off anywhere without saying something to us. Do you think?"

"Who can tell," I said. "With Jolene, who knows."

My mother looked at me as if she thought I had said something profoundly heartless. "She was a very good friend," she said.

"No question about it," I said.

I WAITED all that summer to hear from Jolene, half expecting her to show up at the pool, stick her tongue out at me, and whisper something like, "After work, you and me, we're outta here." But she never came, and in a way I was relieved. I knew I would have gone anywhere she said. I would have left what was turning out to be a fairly normal adolescence after all, high up in my white chair with the zinc oxide on my nose, watching kids swim and splash each other. I would have left it in a second.

I was popular with the younger kids, that summer, for being fair and letting them run off the high dive, but I didn't have a lot to do with kids my own age. I tried to play Jolene's game sometimes, when I got bored, but it never quite worked without her there to set the scenario. The last time I remember trying was sometime toward the end of the summer on a mild, sunny day that smelled just a little like the beginning of fall. It's five years from now, I was telling myself, and you're on a subway in New York. There's a woman across from you who you think might be Jolene, but she's wearing dark glasses and hiding behind a paper. You can't be sure, from what little you see, if it's really her. Now she's staring back at you and she's smiling. Now she's getting up. She's coming toward you and saying something, talking fast.

I remember very clearly trying to imagine what the imaginary woman would say, even closing my eyes to make it clearer; then realizing, suddenly, that I was unable to imagine it because I could no longer remember Jolene at all. I'd forgotten her voice. Nothing was distinct. For a second I was short of breath, trying to figure out where everything had gone. I looked at my hands, opened and closed my fingers a few times and saw the pool through them, blue and sparkling.

Then I looked up and saw two girls my age across from me, burning in the sun and sweating through their towels. One of them rolled onto her stomach. She looked up at me over the tops of her sunglasses, looked away, and said something to her friend. She had short, thick arms and her hips and shoulders were packed with muscles. I could see that her friend had no effect on her whatsoever, on what she had just said or seen, and imagined that her boyfriends, whoever they were, would likely have no real effect either. She caught the elastic of her suit between her thumb and forefinger, tugged it into place, and lay back down with her chin on her hands, her head moving subtly to the beat on the radio between them. That was when it hit me that Jolene was really gone. That was when I knew how long it would be before I ever got past any of this.

DESIRABLE

The fall after Jolene vanished, my mother and I were alone together and caught up in each other's lives as we hadn't been for years. On the anniversary of the day she'd tried to kill herself, we went out. Weeks earlier, I'd promised to be with her, because she said then she might need the support. Afterward she changed her mind, so I was left arguing her old position about sticking together and having someone with her to pass the time, while she said cold-hearted things about never connecting with another human being in the first place. We had Italian food at a place in town, called Benito's, and afterward drove to the top of Onion Mountain, which she said was the best place to see the sunset. Onion Mountain was not really a mountain, but a bald, glorified hill three towns away, where there had been an Indian massacre early in the last century.

We walked a ways to the edge of the sandstone ridge at the top, until the car was out of sight, and sat down facing west, in the grooves of the sandstone that made a kind of natural couch. You could see down a short, gentle ravine into somebody's backyard—a picnic table, a rake, and a bright yellow lawn chair. Beer caps and cigarette butts covered the ground around us and bottles glinted in the underbrush below where partying kids had thrown them.

"Another year. Here I am," she said. "Who would have thought."

"Yes, who would have thought," I said.

She gave me a quizzical look and took a breath like she was going to say something else, but she didn't. Below us a man in a plaid cap appeared, took the rake, and walked back under the trees where we couldn't see him. The light turned the tops of the clouds brown and gold, but it was red going along the horizon and pink where it touched my mother's face and the stone we sat on. You could see the roots of the trees closest to the sandstone, like knuckles, where people had sat and carved their initials and worn away the earth.

"When I was your age," she said, but I wasn't really listening. I'd heard this before. My mother had been a popular girl in high school—captain of cheerleading and voted "best legs" by the football team three years straight. She and her boyfriend, who was a year older, used to drive up Onion Mountain with their friends to neck and drink. Before he graduated, the two of them came up alone one night: he proposed to her, she engraved their initials somewhere in one of the trees, and they stayed up

all night crying about how they would soon have to say
good-bye. Later, when he called her from college to dump
her for another girl, she drove up with some friends,
drunk, and gouged out the letters with a hunting knife.
"All my girlhood dreams down the drain, like that," she
said. "My big first heartbreak."

"Think how much worse it would be if you actually
married the guy," I said.

"Of course. But then you might have a father at least,
and that would be something." She laughed. "Only, you
wouldn't be you at all. You'd be some other kid—Virginia
or Hollis."

"Very funny," I said.

"It is. It's funny." She got out a cigarette and rolled it
back and forth between her fingers. "I don't understand.
Here I tell you all this stuff and I don't have the first idea
what goes on in your private life."

"Why would you want to know about that?"

She shrugged. "Because I'm your mother."

We were silent awhile after that, both of us watching
the sun go down and the light dying around us. Then she
lit the cigarette and put her hand on my knee a second,
breathing in smoke. "I'm sorry for being so negative back
there in the restaurant," she said, talking the smoke out.
"I'm much better now. What I said to you, about people
never knowing how to help each other. You know what I
meant, don't you?"

"Yes," I said. "I think so." I told her I'd thought about it before, because I'd often noticed that when you're feeling unhappy, people will avoid you—although being alone is the last thing in the world you need.

"Right, but that's not what I meant," she said. "It's just the other way around, in fact, because when you try to help, that's when you don't manage to connect with anybody."

There was nothing for me to say to this. It was getting dark now, the night shapes of the trees coming out around us like objects stranded from their real selves. I worried about how we would find our way back to the parking lot in the dark and kept going over that in my mind, escaping across the sandstone, leaving her here or holding her up on one arm. I scraped my foot against the stone and leaned back on the heels of my hands, looking out where there was still a stripe of light left, where the sun had disappeared.

"I want you to know what happened last year," she said.

I felt a kind of paralysis, like my blood had stopped— like what I used to feel sometimes when I was with Jolene. "You told me. When you were in the hospital, you kept telling me," I said.

She rubbed out her cigarette on the rock and flicked it away. "Charlie, I still need to talk things out. Not that all of it makes sense. But you need to let me talk."

"Talk to your shrink."

"This isn't something I need to say to her. I need to say it to you."

I shook my head. "No. You were depressed. You wanted your life to be better than it was and you couldn't see how to change it, so you tried to kill yourself."

There was a silence. "Fine," she said calmly. "If you don't care what I have to tell you, I'm not going to try." She stood and held out a hand to help me up. "Let's go." She was in a blue windbreaker and thin black cotton pants that fit close to her legs. Her hair had grown out almost to her shoulders. The way she looked, standing over me in the half-light, it occurred to me what an attractive woman she must be. There was a looseness about her—a flexibility in her hips, like an offer that negated itself the moment it was given, leaving you completely to blame for however you took it and whatever you made of her. I thought, If I was another person this is the way I would have to look at her. "I'd like to do something for you, Charlie," she said as she pulled me up.

"Like what?"

"Something nice." She dropped my hand and smoothed the front of her pants straight, looking at me. "Name it," she said. "A favor—a reasonable favor. Any kind."

"I don't know what you're getting at."

"I'm not getting at anything."

"What kind of favor are you talking about?"

"For crying out loud. You have no imagination, kid. Like, how about we say I'll buy you a couple of six-packs and then we'll go find your friends, whoever they are, and you can have a night with them. Stagger home drunk. It's Friday. There must be something interesting going on. Right? What do you say?"

"I think that would be very nice of you."

"See," she said, walking quickly away from me, "I'm not all bad." I went after her with a feeling that I was floating across the sandstone. I couldn't see where to put my feet. I felt the stored heat of the day coming up around my knees and soaking through the soles of my shoes.

AT THE supermarket we got two six-packs of Molson beer. "For my alcoholic son," she said to the checker, who looked about my age. He had yellow hair and acne, and he was trying hard to seem unfrightened by what she said, though I could see it wouldn't fit anywhere in his mind. I could tell from the way he kept looking at me.

"Why do you have to say things like that?" I asked her. I looked right at the checker. "It's a joke. That's her idea of a funny joke," I said.

She laughed, snapped her purse shut, and headed for the door.

"It's so uncool. He might have been someone I know," I said, struggling alongside, the beer in a plastic bag that swung against my leg. We went through the electric doors and back out across the parking lot.

"Listen, Charlie," she said. "I'm sorry it disturbs you, but I'll say whatever I please."

"Wonderful news."

Now I had a feeling like we were a couple on a last, vicious date—the way she slammed her door still smiling at me and then leaned across the seat inside to unlock mine.

"Where to?" she asked, as we went out of the parking lot.

"Rob Landau's—first right on Woodberry Lane," I said. "Jake Hamer said something about maybe going over there tonight for poker."

She moved the package of beer between us on the seat a little closer to her leg, then took one out and opened it. "Is this a regular kind of thing—the guys getting together and playing cards?" she asked. She had a swig of beer and tucked the bottle between her legs.

"No," I said. "Yes and no. It happens sometimes. It happens when it happens."

She waved a hand at me. "Never mind, I won't pry," she said. "So male."

"What's wrong with that?"

"Just about everything in the world."

At Landau's house I picked out Jake's VW parked at an odd angle on the corner of the street. I pointed at it and said, "Yeah, there's Jake."

She stopped the car. Through Landau's front picture window I saw Mr. Landau, who was bald and wiry, on a flower-patterned couch in the gold light, reading a magazine. He had a look on his face like something infuriated him. Then Rob's stepmother came into the room and walked past him. She was in a pink sweatshirt that stretched almost to her knees. He looked up at her and the anger went out of his face, then she said something and he said something back.

"She's going to bed now," my mother whispered, as if they might hear. "She won't ask him to come with her because she doesn't think she should have to. And he doesn't know what she's not asking for, but he knows she wants something and he's not going to let her have it because she's bothering him. Stalemate."

"What?" I asked.

She nodded. "Any fool can see."

"Sure," I said. I unlatched the car door and pushed it open. "I'll be home sometime late tonight, I don't know when. Maybe Jake will stay over. Probably he will, if I ask him." I had one foot on the curb and the car door was chiming.

"Hmm," she said. She turned off the motor. "On second thought, I think I'll just go in for a second and say hi— be sure they know I gave my son that alcohol to drink."

"Then let's go."

"Wait, wait," she said. She got out some breath freshener and squirted it on her tongue, then bounced her hair out around her ears, looking in the rearview mirror. "Here comes the homewrecker," she said and made a face at herself, dropping the breath freshener back in her bag and snapping it shut.

"What?" I said.

She blinked at me and smiled. "Oh, it's just a word. A line from a movie. Or a song. I forget which."

"Wait a minute. What are you about to do?" I asked.

She was still smiling. "Nothing, nothing," she said.

I asked her again as we went across the street. "What are you going to do?"

She held out a mostly full bottle of beer at me. "Here. Do you want the rest?"

I shook my head. "Mr. Landau is not the nicest guy in the world," I said. "In fact he's kind of a jerk."

"Not to worry," she said. She bent and stuck the beer bottle in a clump of grass next to the sidewalk, then hurried to catch up. "Never anticipate a situation with your bad will, Charlie—you'll only create the thing you don't wish for."

We rang the bell and waited for Mr. Landau. It was a few minutes before he answered. When he looked at her I knew that anything she had in mind for him was probably going to work.

"Why not?" he said about the beer. "Long as everyone's safe here at home. I don't care. They're all down in the basement."

"Excuse me," I said, and I went by, leaving them there in the doorway saying whatever it was they found to say to each other.

ROB LANDAU was really Jake's friend, not mine. They were both seniors and had known each other since grade school, skipped classes together through junior high, and spent two summers on Cape Cod running a campground maintenance crew. I thought they were a perfect pair, Rob in his Top-Siders and preppy button-collar shirts that didn't match his Jewish face, Jake with his thin beard and his ripped, rich-kid hippy clothes. I became friends with them when Rob, who was editor-in-chief of the school newspaper, assigned Jake and me to cowrite an article supporting Jimmy Carter's first run for the presidency. Jake did most of the research and I did the writing. There were things in that article I had no way to prove and took on absolute faith—Jake was that convincing, and I needed friends that badly. In the picture of us that went into print with the article we are holding up a disembodied car bumper covered with Carter stickers. Jake has his tongue out and he's jumping up and down in place to stay warm, so it looks as if he's about to disappear, while I'm staring straight at the camera, my eyebrows tight-

ening into each other and a look on my face like I can't
figure anything out.

Our game went until almost two in the morning.
Aside from the beer I'd brought there was a pint of peach
brandy, some schnapps, and a fifth of Southern Comfort—enough to get five teenagers (Rob, Jake, and two of
their friends, Tim Dietz and Dennis Witherspoon) drunk
to the point of saying stupid things and carrying on—
even Jake, who was quiet and reserved most of the time.
That night he was obsessed by a girl who didn't know
who he was, and would most likely never care if she did.
"Melissa," he said. "I insist," he looked at me, "the first and
last miracle of God is a girl, sixteen, stripped to the waist."

"No kidding," I said.

"That's poetry," he said. "A poet wrote that." He pointed
at me. "He has the same name as you, Charlie, so you
should feel especially moved by it."

"I don't," I said.

"Well, you should."

"Hamer, shut up a second, I'm trying to deal—what
do you want?" Rob asked me. I held up two fingers.

"How about this," Jake said. "I want to suck the honey
from her mellifluent melliferousness." His gray eyes were
jumping around on something behind me. "It's good,
huh? Mellifluent melliferousness. Honey in her veins so
when you lick her tits it tastes like candy. When she
sweats . . . no, when she stands out in the rain," he

looked at the ceiling, then back at me, "it smells like melons."

"That's nice, Jake," I said. "You have some imagination."

But his attention was on Rob now. "Fold," he said, and put his cards facedown on the table. He pushed his chair back behind him. "Anyway, I have to piss."

"That girl was in my Western civ class last year," Rob said, after Jake was gone. "She is like the dumbest person I've ever met. Didn't know who Mussolini was."

"I hear every word you're saying, Landau!" Jake yelled from the bathroom. "Whatever you're saying, I hear it."

Rob looped a finger in the air next to his head. "The guy's touched."

We helped Jake think of strategies for making Melissa notice him. The only thing to save it from being depressing was Jake himself, who was ridiculous instead of sad and kept managing to transform his lack of appeal to a thing you might actually prefer. He was not bad looking, but he was a little strange. He had a long face with features that seemed to be running away from themselves. The beard didn't hide that. His shoulders were narrow, the right one coming up an inch or two higher than the left so he always appeared to be carrying something.

The night ended with some stupidly serious moments brought on by the one kid everyone liked least, Tim Dietz, who was always saying things about what great friends we were. That night it was a matter of going around the table, each of us taking a turn at predicting where we'd be in ten years, and everything we hoped for in life. It had the unnerving solemnity of pact-making and there was that awful pact-making silence that went with it.

"A famous psychiatrist," Jake said. "I specialize in treating women. Beautiful ones. Fucked-up beautiful women." His tongue went across his lips. "They pay me to keep figuring them out and I listen to all their problems, and it's a wonderful arrangement."

"Tonight I have no idea," was what I said. I thought about the boy who had escaped my mother when she was my age, and tried to imagine his life now. "No, I have an idea," I said. "In ten years I'll be very rich. I'll have a house with twenty-five rooms in it and a white picket fence and a pool in back. Hundreds of acres of land. No wife, no kids. Different girlfriends all over the world, wherever I do business." The room was peculiarly silent. "Shit, I don't know."

"No, no, that's beautiful." It was Tim, being too sincere. I stared at him and thought he only got away with being as earnest as he was because of his glasses and asthma. No one could hurt him. Jake flashed me a knowing look, fished his keys out of his pocket, and started snapping them around his fingers, into the palm of his hand.

AT HOME there were two glasses of orange juice on the kitchen counter and four aspirin between them. A note from my mother said: "Boys, Nights like this I can't believe what a LUCKY person I am I'm still alive. I'll tell you all about it in the morning. YOU DRINK UP SO YOU DON'T HAVE A HANGOVER IN THE AM. XOX. Mother."

"What a twit," I said.

"I think your mom's okay," Jake said. "She's funny at least, you know. It's probably better having someone like her than my mother."

"Someone like her—what do you mean?"

"Weird," he said. He looked into his glass and stretched his eyebrows higher into his long, dentless forehead, and shrugged. "Yeah. Weird," he said.

"What's weird?"

"Fucked-up."

We took our aspirin and drank our orange juice and left the glasses in the sink. In the living room I pointed out the beam next to the stairs and we stood under it for a few minutes, looking up. "The scene of the crime," Jake said. My mother had told him all about her suicide attempt the first time he came over with a store of Jimmy Carter facts. "I'd be pissed as hell if it was my mom who tried to kill herself."

"You would?"

"Yeah, I would." He was staring at me.

"Why?"

"For doing it."

We went into the den in back and watched TV. There was a documentary on about snakes and the different ways they kill their prey. I sat on the floor with Jake behind me on the sofa until I heard him snoring. Then I went upstairs. I wondered if he really dreamed about Melissa and the honey in her veins, or if that was just a romantic pretense to keep us laughing, and I tried to imagine how it would feel to have all your illusions still intact, like Jake—thinking of girls as sugary, unknown concoctions. I was in the hall outside my mother's room when I was thinking all this, and suddenly I was remembering Jolene. I saw her bare shoulders in my mind and knew exactly what her skin felt like and where my hands fit on her. I heard the way she said my name. I continued down the hall and into my room, found my bed in the dark because I didn't want to see anything, stripped, and threw myself down to sleep.

JAKE WAS already awake when I came downstairs, his hair a mass of brown, wet curls that covered his neck and stained the collar of his T-shirt with water. He was sitting over a plate of scrambled eggs and eating with his fingers while my mother, across from him, smoked a cigarette and watched. There was music on in the living room to drown out what was not being said between them. "Charlie," she said, and stood up. She stood crookedly, and right away I knew she had something to hide—the way she looked at me, then away, then back again with some defiance. She frowned and leaned over her chair. She was in a thin blue bathrobe and slippers.

"Morning," I said. I pressed a hand to my temple. The room was too hot and the smoke stung my sinuses.

Jake kept picking up pieces of scrambled egg with his fingers and putting them in his mouth, chewing with his front teeth and swallowing. He took a sip of orange juice and smirked. "Morning," he said. "Feeling it a little?"

"A little," I said.

"Some hair of the dog?" my mother asked. "Or just coffee?" I knew what it was she had to hide then. She was sitting across the table from my best friend, getting him drunk and watching him eat with his fingers. It was harmless, on the one hand, but on the other hand it was chilling. She said, "Oh I know you like an old song. Mr. Straight-and-Narrow. Coffee it is." She turned around and started swinging cupboards open and shut, taking out dishes for me and grinding coffee, talking about Mr. Landau the whole time. I wasn't able to concentrate. She kept referring to him as "the man with money," and asked me if I knew how well off he'd be if he didn't have to pay maintenance on those two other wives.

"No," I said. "How well off?"

"Six times as much money. He's a Ph.D., you know, not an actual medical doctor," she said. "He does research over at the pharmaceutical plant on Belvedere. Actually, we have lots in common, as it turns out."

"Look," I said, finally, just to shut her up. "I don't care. What you said, you know . . . you don't know me. In fact, you don't know me at all."

Jake stopped chewing. He narrowed his eyes at me and shook his head, then looked at my mother.

"There's no reason to pick a fight with me about this, Charlie. Nothing happened."

"I never said anything happened, did I. I said you don't know me. You said you knew me. I said you don't. You don't know me like you said you do." For a while after that I was conscious of things blurring nicely as the throbbing in my head stopped. I stared at the table and watched Jake eating and was unable to remove my attention from that. The table was covered by a white tablecloth and there were three full settings, a pitcher of orange juice in the middle, which I now imagined to be laced with vodka, several bottles of vitamins, and a small octagonal basket of textured paper napkins with yellow flowers on them. "Why do you always eat with your fingers?" I asked Jake.

Jake looked up at me and smiled so his beard stuck out at the bottom. "I like to," he said. "It feels more real. I don't have to."

My mother spun around to face us. "Does it really bother you that much if I'm friendly with Rob's father?" she asked. "Because if it's going to be such a problem, then I won't have anything more to do with him. You just say the word." She spoke firmly, finishing with a smile, though I could see she wasn't a bit relaxed.

"You should do whatever it is you want," I said. "It's not really all that interesting to me."

THE LIGHT was soaked and blurry, like twilight all day, and the air was charged with a kind of seasonal tumult— unusually warm, but with the feeling of warmth that won't last. We went to Jake's house a few miles out of town and ended up playing two-on-two tackle with his neighbors Simon and Emil in Jake's backyard next to the swimming pool, which was full of dead leaves that blackened the water. Simon and Emil were better players, but we beat them because we were more aggressive and had a sense of humor while they did not. Whenever Simon dropped something Emil threw at him they would call each other names in Hebrew and English and then push each other around for a while. We thought it was funny and tried doing it ourselves, but that only made them stop and stare coldly at us, without understanding.

Afterward I lay on my back on the slate that went around the swimming pool. I was out of breath and full of feelings I had no way to understand. The air turned cold on me, drying the sweat in my clothes and sticking my hair to my forehead. The wind rattled in the little leaves of the poplars and ashes and moose maples lining the back of Jake's yard, churning the late-day light as it went across us. I wanted to say something about this to Jake, but I didn't think he would understand. So I got up and said, "Let's go."

We went inside, ate some spaghetti, and drank beer watching TV, because his mother wasn't home. Later we walked by a jock party and stood outside listening to kids chant, "Toga, toga, toga." Then we went to the college, where we climbed up the field house roof and sat with our legs over the edge, spitting down onto the ground and getting dizzy. After a while Jake lay back so I could only see him from the corner of my eye. I looked over my knees and imagined dropping forward until my teeth ached from it and my knees were numb.

"So what's this stuff about Melissa?" I asked.

"What stuff?"

"You know. Last night. What you were saying." I knew vaguely who Melissa was—a short girl with winged-back blond hair and pert features. She'd dated the captain of the hockey team for years before he graduated high school. Now, with him gone, she was alone all the time instead of walking around on his arm or carrying one handle of his gym bag. I pictured her in white carpenter pants, tennis shoes, and a preppy sweater.

"She's gorgeous," Jake said seriously. He propped himself on his elbows. "Fucking perfect."

"She's nice," I said.

"Understatement of the year."

"Hey," I said. "Did something happen? Did you ask her out?"

He snorted. "Nothing like that."

"Come on. Tell it."

"Nothing to tell."

"Whatever it is Jake, you can trust me. I want you to know. I wouldn't say anything to anyone."

"Oh sure," he said.

I scooted back from the edge of the roof and sat cross-legged next to him, then I lay back too, so our heads were inches apart. I could smell beer and spaghetti on his breath. I wanted his pleasure for myself—the possibility of this girl with blond hair and everything he made of her. I said, "I want you to feel like I'm somebody you could talk to."

"Very nice of you, dear," he said. He licked one finger and tried to stick it in my ear but I was too quick for him.

We stayed awhile longer, laughing at things that weren't funny and staring at the sky, which was dull and starless from the lights of town. I kept thinking about a movie I'd seen where two astronauts are stranded in a broken rocketship in outer space, sharing one oxygen tank. In the end there are some very gripping scenes where the two men are floating outside their capsule in the dark, slowly dying of oxygen depletion, sweating and writhing in their spacesuits and gasping selfish things to each other through their headsets. A Russian cosmonaut arrives just in time to pump them back up with air and bring them home. When news of the rescue reaches NASA headquarters everyone starts rejoicing, throwing things in the air and shouting.

Later we walked back to Jake's house, where I slept on some couch pillows on the living room floor. All night I dreamed I was falling. I kept waking up and sleeping again. I dreamed I was falling over the edge of the field house roof and Simon and Emil were running around trying to catch me. I dreamed I was falling through tree-tops that didn't touch me. Then I was in an elevator that went down so fast my feet came off the floor.

IN THE morning, my mother was desperate for me to come home. "Please, Charlie, something terrible has happened."

"What," I said. "What happened?"

"I can't possibly tell you over the phone. Please just come home. Where have you been all night?"

"At Jake's," I said.

"Thank God! You didn't see Rob at all last night?"

This could mean only one thing. I tried to picture her with Mr. Landau, but that was impossible. There was the resonant tick of a grandfather clock in the next room where Jake's mother was having coffee and reading the paper, waiting for Jake and me. I heard her clear her throat once. "No. I'm just going to take a shower and then I'll probably have something to eat, then I'll have Jake drive me home," I said. "I just woke up."

"Charlie! How long? How long is it going to take you?"

"An hour. Forty-five minutes. Just . . ." I couldn't think of what to tell her to do with herself until I got there. "I'll be there, okay?"

"You disappoint me," she said.

"I don't mean to," I said.

"But you do."

"I'll be home as soon as I can," I said, but she had already hung up.

Jake wanted to come. He said it could be like his first opportunity to deal with someone in a real crisis. I shook my head. I knew there was no real crisis. He was peeling an orange, the juice misting around his fingers in little bursts. We sat across from each other at the dining room table, which was elegantly laid out. Jake's mother didn't believe in eating casually. Even breakfast had to be done with cloth napkins in silver rings, and monogrammed flatware, and bowls of bread and fruit arranged for the best balance of color. I thought it was no wonder Jake liked eating with his fingers when he wasn't at home.

"But I really think I could help," Jake said. "Me and your mother have like this understanding."

"No you don't, Jake." I shook my head again. "I'll take notes. I'll tell you all about it."

"It's not the same as being there." He grinned. "You

don't know how much you really want me there. You want me there, you just don't know it."

His mother came out of the kitchen with a platter of baked eggs on English muffins covered in thick white sauce. She looked nothing like Jake—small and trim with flat gray-blond hair. Maybe around the eyes and nose there was something similarly piercing and humorous. She was an architect and her hands had a bewitching kind of calmness and symmetry, whichever way she moved them, like they were the ideal extension of her innermost thoughts. I'd seen her read and knit and listen to an opera at the same time, never breaking concentration.

She sat at the head of the table and started interviewing Jake about his classes and everything he had done during the week. The sauce covering the eggs was surprisingly tart and chalky and had bits of pimiento in it. I didn't like it, but I kept eating. I tried to imagine Jake and his mother hadn't seen each other all week, and maybe this was why she had so many questions. Jake sat forward in his seat and I worried that things would jump out of his hands. His plate was too close to the edge of the table. He slurped his orange juice and set it back down noisily. I almost never saw him use silverware and he didn't seem very good at it, although he was managing. His mother was particularly interested in the AP physics class he was taking, and seemed pleased with him for his description of something he had learned about radiant bodies and an equation for measuring distance between redshifted galaxies.

"Yes. Distance is time!" she said. She held her hands apart to demonstrate. "The farther out we see, the further back in time, the better we know ourselves and the origins of everything."

Jake shook his head, talking and chewing at the same time. "There's stuff out there nobody knows what the hell it is." He gestured with his fork. "Galaxies flying apart faster than the speed of light . . ."

His mother cleared her throat and glanced at her watch. It was one of those watches with no numbers on it. "How are your studies, Charlie?" she asked. "You never say anything."

I felt trapped and completely transparent. I imagined there could be nothing in my head possibly worth offering her. "Fine. Fine," I said.

"Two days until your man has his shot at the presidency," she said. "I'll bet you're glad—it looks as if you'll win."

Jake stood up. "Charlie has to get home. What did your mother say the problem was?" He pushed his chair into the table.

"She didn't," I said.

"Addicts never do," his mother said. I stared at her and couldn't believe she had said that. She smiled and I noticed how perfectly tan her cheeks were, but I also noticed the lines in them. I didn't see how a surface could be this smooth and broken at the same time. "It's not *what* she needs, it's *that* she needs, period. Jake, you can leave the cleanup till you get back. Guess you won't have any help." She moved the newspaper that was folded in quarters next to her into view and then traced her index finger down the column of print until she'd found the word where she'd left off.

IN OUR house it was warm and smelled like cigarette smoke and burned bacon. The light was dull coming through the dirty front picture window. The boards popped under my feet as I turned to kick my shoes off and shut the front door. I heard my mother's voice in the kitchen. I missed the first part of what she said because I thought she was talking to me and figured she would only repeat herself. But she didn't. She went on, and I realized there was someone else in there she was talking to, and she didn't know I had returned home. I heard low male laughter.

"Ha!" my mother said. "A year ago Friday. Honest to God!"

I remembered something about her the way she was before the suicide attempt, before the antidepressants. It was a strange memory that had to do with a postcard I'd gotten in the mail from my father, who was then in Spain. My mother kept it to herself for days and when she gave it to me she apologized profusely, saying she had realized she couldn't protect me from him or his kind of influence, and it was just as well that way. I couldn't see what she was worked up about. It wasn't like I'd known the postcard was missing, or like I got such a great number of them that missing one for a few days was going to set me back in a treasured correspondence I had with the man. "Just take it," she said. On the back of the card he had written something like "Down the coast from here for the big month of April. Keep up the good work, Son. Lovingly, your father."

But this is not what I remembered. What I remembered is coming into the living room and finding her there alone, doing absolutely nothing, just staring, with the postcard next to her on the couch—and the anger in her that was a kind of blackness or paralysis, and how I felt that and understood it at once and knew it was real.

"Actually," my mother continued, "I was pretty gone that day." There was silence in the kitchen, and even where I was standing I could feel the tension snap tight around what she said. "Eight in the morning, blotto— you know what that's like?" she asked. Lie, I thought. She hardly drank in those days.

The man said "hmm" and "ahh," or maybe he didn't actually say it, but it was what I felt implied in the silence.

She said, "I called in sick—back then I had plenty of sick days coming." I went quietly through the living room and halfway up the stairs, where I stopped, turned around, and sat down. It was Mr. Landau. He was sitting at the kitchen table with his legs crossed and his hands folded in his lap. The light was a fist of white knuckles on the top of his bald head. He was wearing yellow sweats, a turtleneck with a torn sweatshirt over it, and jogging shoes. From where I sat I thought I could smell him—a mixture of citrus-smelling aftershave, soap, and sweat. She must have wanted me to get here before he arrived, to help prevent her from letting anything further happen between the two of them.

She said, "It was an accident. I swear to God, I had a headache and I wanted to get rid of it. It just didn't quite work like I thought. For crying out loud. I slipped."

He chuckled and then rubbed a hand on the back of his neck. "No," he said.

"I was drunk! What do you expect?"

"Honestly."

She started banging her hand on a counter and making the dishes jump. "It was like that. Just this throb-bing pain, I've never had it before, like everything was so fucked-up and lousy and worthless and my head hurt so much all I wanted was to cut it off. Cut out everything. So I thought I'd just stop the circulation a little—slow things down. You know that old Marx Brothers movie where they tie the guy's tooth to the doorknob and slam it shut."

"Mary, I just can't believe . . . ," Mr. Landau said. He swung his head back and forth. "If I'd been there . . . "

"Oh, Marrion," she said. "Stop. You're going to make me wish you hadn't come." She went and stood in front of him, then put her hands on his face and drew him into her stomach. His arms went around her waist.

I got up then, turned, and meant to head quietly upstairs to my room, where I'd just get on with my homework, or something else, and try not to feel the disgust that was slowly turning the center of my mind to nothing. But I wasn't careful enough or I wasn't thinking. Or I wanted to be found out. Anyway, I fell. I went down on my knees with a thump, caught myself hard on my hands, then straightened up and kept going. I saw her behind me as I stood up, or maybe I just felt her there, staring after me.

"Charlie," she said. "Charlie. What the—where are you going?"

I slammed the door at the end of the upstairs hall and never said a word to her about it.

MY MOTHER never took any pleasure in being beautiful, that I knew. She never said anything about it, never looked happily in a mirror touching the parts of her face that pleased people to see. As far as I could tell she was like a person who hated herself to death. Men were lucky and dangerous cards she had been dealt to play. It was hard for me to understand at times, because obviously there was more than luck involved. The men were not static; they had opinions of their own. They were not dealt, they were drawn. They came and went. They had ideas about her, and most of those ideas leaned toward one thing: they thought she was desirable. For me it was a matter of always having to look at the same thing from two sides. There was my mother, who could never see the beauty in herself, and there was the man, who could see only beauty. Then there was beauty itself—a vague, slipped-over territory where they fought to define themselves and be understood.

Outside it began snowing lightly. I heard my mother laugh once, and this is when I knew I had to leave. I didn't want to know what she was doing anymore. I went downstairs, out through the side door, into the garage, and back outside with my bicycle. I had no idea where I was headed, or how long I'd be gone. I had on a sweater, a shirt, and jeans—not enough to stay warm, but that was all right as long as I kept moving. I pedaled until the things I could think about were my breath going in and out, and my front tire rolling on the wet pavement. The snow stuck for seconds on the backs of my hands. Water flew off my rear tire, making a stripe of cold up my back.

Eventually I went to Jake's. No one was home so I walked around in back to sit on an old metal chair that apparently didn't warrant being stored for the winter. The metal made my legs cold at first, but that didn't last. I watched the snow settle over the grass and the dead leaves of the hibiscus plant growing in the trellis next to me and the trees all around, and I thought about summer. The snow was a constant hiss that tickled the insides of my ears and didn't leave me any feelings of peace. The pool showed a reflection of their house and some of the trees behind me, but it kept being dimpled and broken apart by the huge snowflakes. I tried to imagine my mother waking up alone after however long it was she'd lain on the living room floor with her leg broken and I wondered what made her drag herself to the phone to call for help.

Jake appeared at the other side of the pool. He grinned and shook his head. "God damn," he said.

"What?" I asked.

"Bad news." He pulled his shirt off over his head, and his flesh turned to goosebumps. He beat his fists on his chest. It made a thin, slapping sound that seemed much less than it should have been. "Time for a swim," he said. He kicked his shoes off, unzipped his pants, and hopped from foot to foot, tugging the legs down. His belt jingled and some change fell from his pockets onto the damp slate.

"You're a crazy nut, Jake," I said. "Are you sober?"

"Very much so," he said. And a second later he dived into the green-black water. He came up yelping, his hair stuck to his head and his beard running with water. He swam for the edge of the pool, kicked off, that and went back across to the platform where the diving board used to be. "Not so bad," he said. "*L'eau est délicieuse*. Oh my God! I think there's fucking fish in here." He pulled himself up on the edge of the pool but didn't get out. "She told me I'm crazy," he said. "Melissa," he said, when he saw I didn't know what he was talking about. "I went to her house today to see if she knew who I was and everything, and she said I'm crazy. Fucking ran away like I was threatening her. Can you believe it?" He yipped and dropped backward into the water, swam to the other side of the pool, then disappeared.

I was alone and too aware of myself, my inaction, standing there with my hands on my hips, narrowing my eyes at the murky water that had no real reflection left in it, only the broken places where light jumped off. The snow had nearly stopped. "Come on, come on," I said. And the next time he came up I ran around the pool to where he was and got him by the hair. "Hey!" he yelled. His hair was ropy and thick and stuck between my fingers. I pulled until he screamed at me to stop, then I got him under the arms and lifted until my face was against his and I could hear his teeth clacking wildly and his breath going in and out. "Man oh man, it's cold," he said. "Oh man. I've never been this cold. Jesus." He convulsed and the shivers jerked back through me.

"That's better," he said, his hands slipping on mine. "Much better."

"You'll be all right."

"You think so," he said.

"Yeah, you will."

"I have to tell you everything she said to me."

"No you don't. Not now," I said and I pushed him away, across the lawn. "Get in there and take a hot shower. You hear me?" He scampered ahead on his toes, naked, hugging himself, up the back steps and across the deck. "Hot as you can stand it," I said.

He stopped at the door and turned around, crouched almost double with his hands clasped at his crotch, shivering. His lips were swollen and blue. Stuff was running out of his nose and I could see the movement of his muscles under his skin, like lizards and tongues. He tried to thank me. He said, "I'm glad you were here," and then something else about giving me a ride home, but he was shaking so badly he couldn't really speak.

"This is ridiculous!" I yelled. "Get in there!"

He nodded. "Okay. Just . . . thanks," he said.

"Go!" I yelled, and he went inside.

SHE LOOKED up when I came in the door. She said, "Charlie, good lord." Already it was night. I stared until her image on the couch, lying in the shadows, was like something superimposed on my vision: a shape in a bathrobe that opened to her stomach; feet in pink socks one over the other; head turned toward me. "Where in hell have you been?"

"Nowhere," I said.

"We need to have a little talk, don't we?"

"I have nothing to say to you," I said, and it was true. "I want to eat some dinner."

"Excuse me for living," she said.

"Just get off me about that stuff," I said. "Whether or not you live is your own fucking business. It doesn't depend on a single thing aside from that."

She had a Kleenex tucked in one hand. Now she uncurled it and rubbed it nervously under her nose. "You would just shut me out like that, wouldn't you?"

"Shut you out like what?"

"Like what you just said."

"No," I said. "No. I'm not shutting you out. I'm going to heat up some soup in the kitchen, because I'm hungry."

She pulled herself upright, hugging the robe around her, and slid her feet into slippers, then raked her fingers back through her hair and groaned. "Oh," she said. She buried her face in her hands momentarily, then took them away and said, "You sit. I'll get us something nice."

I followed her into the kitchen and sat at the table where Mr. Landau had been. I picked up the salt shaker, which was shaped to look like a blond farmboy in overalls, singing. Before it wore off, the paint around his eyes had shown what a happy boy he was, singing, his face upturned to catch the light in his eyes and cheeks. I tipped it over in my palm. A trickle of salt ran out and stopped. I shook it and more salt sprinkled into my palm. I turned the shaker right side up and put it next to its mate, then licked the salt out of my palm, wincing at the fierce taste, and rubbed my hand off on my jeans. "So what's the story with Marrion Landau?" I asked.

"No story," she said.

"And I'm the prince of France."

"Let's just put it like this—you won't be seeing him around here again," she said. "That's a promise." She cut the vegetable knife up and down through the halves of an onion. The smell of it came across the kitchen at me.

"Good," I said. "And have you decided to stop wishing your life was different than it is?"

She kept cutting, sniffed, and ran a hand under her nose. "I don't know what you're talking about."

"No?"

"No."

I crossed one leg over the other and watched her. It was like seeing something come apart. First she turned the wrong way, dropping the lid of the frying pan; then she jumped at the noise and covered her ears too late. Her eyes and nose were running from the onion. She saw that the vegetables she had cut were in uneven pieces, too big or too small—tomatoes, potatoes, onion, pepper—

and started cutting the pieces into more pieces. She threw a fistful of peels at the trash and missed, grazed the back of her finger grating zest of lemon, then threw the grater at the sink. It bounced and flew up into the air, spinning, and landed on the floor.

"I can't," she said. "I just can't do it." She sat across the table from me, her face hidden behind her hands, and began to cry. There were pepper seeds and bits of tomato skin stuck on the backs of her fingers. She made so much noise crying, the air gusting in and out of her, at first I didn't believe it. And when she began speaking her voice was too loud, as if it wouldn't fit the words she wanted to say. "I didn't mean to get things so screwed up for you, all right? I just wanted to have a good time. I deserve a good time once in a while." She sniffed hard and wiped her cheeks, then went on more calmly. "And anyway, nobody knows but you—you and me and him. Your friend Rob has no idea."

"So what?"

She sniffed again. "What do you mean, so what?" She sounded as if she might laugh at me.

"I mean, I don't give a damn who knows or doesn't know."

"Oh, I see. It's just so disgusting to you, the very idea I might have some sexual feelings, it doesn't matter to you who I sleep with, as long as you don't know about it. Right?"

I shook my head. "It was wrong, Mom. Plain and

simple. You don't sleep with your son's friend's father, who also happens to be married. You just don't. And you didn't do it because you had some uncontrollable sexual feelings, either. I don't buy that for a second. You did it because you can't leave me alone. You can't *be* alone."

"That . . . ," she began, and stopped. She took a few breaths. "You are the cruelest young man I know. The *cruelest*," she yelled, and I felt the warmth of her breath and saliva all over my face. She covered her eyes again and began to sob.

"No, I'm not," I said. I put my hands on top of hers, gently pulled them away from her face and out into the middle of the table. Her face was red and streaked from crying. "I'm not saying that to be cruel. Not at all. I'm just telling you I don't think it was right."

"Let me go," she said, and I did.

She went back to the sink, where she ran water into a glass and drank it, then stood for a long time, all her weight on one leg, looking out into the dark. She turned to face me and there was a kind of blindedness in the way she stared. She gestured at the counters. "This mess. Just leave it till morning. I can't do a thing about it. I'm going to bed now. Sorry about your dinner." She went out of the room, holding one hand on her forehead.

When she was gone I dumped all the vegetables she had cut into one pot, poured in some tomato sauce, olive oil, and wine and let it cook. I sat down at the table and tried to arrange everything I knew about myself, but it didn't take long for me to see that it couldn't be done. I wanted there to be someone across the table from me, listening, and I wanted to say how completely ridiculous I thought it was that I was alive. Of course there was no one. And even if there had been someone, the thing I wanted to say would not go through: either I wouldn't dare say it, I'd have something else to say, or the person I said it to wouldn't care. Realizing this I began to feel easier inside. The invisible person across from me, instead of seeming less believable, seemed more so.

"Jake is just a kid," I said to him. "He wouldn't be able to help." I pictured Jake running across the lawn on his toes, naked, his shoulders hunched. "I couldn't ask him for help." I rubbed my hands all over my face. My skin felt dry and itched badly underneath. Then I looked around the room. Everything was jumping out at me. "I have a lot of work to do," I said out loud, and there was a despairing quality to my voice, because it was true. I hadn't touched a textbook all weekend. I wanted to see myself getting up from the table with a big pot of coffee to carry upstairs to my room, where I'd spend the rest of the night happily poring over chapters of history and solving trig problems. But I wasn't going anywhere. "What kind of help would you ask for, anyway?" I asked myself. "What kind?" I answered. "What a ridiculous question. The kind I *need*." I made a fist and put it on the table. The heat came on then and I felt warm air blow across my face.

I remembered a weekend Jolene and I had spent together, when she painted her fingernails and toenails bright, plastic pink. It was a bad weekend, toward the end of our time together. She kept taking her clothes on and off to show the polish in contrast to her natural skin color and to prove to me that nail polish is actually intended to make you think of a person naked. She said, "This is what you'll miss about me, when I'm gone," and lifted one foot, flexed, into my face, her toenails gleaming like little pink bugs.

I pushed back from the table and held my breath. I didn't want to be thinking about Jolene. Certainly I needed something, but it wasn't her anymore. "Jolene," I said. "No!" And I got up from the table, started pacing back and forth across the kitchen. I ran my hands over the counters. I touched everything I saw—cupboard handles, silverware handles shining in the dish drainer, a crusty plaid potholder hanging next to the stove, spice jars that were waxy with dirt, the chipped edges of plates. I opened the refrigerator, looked in, and shut it.

I opened the back door and looked out into the night, and tried to remember what it had felt like when I was a kid and believed my mother was someone to take care of me. I remembered being in a field with her somewhere, lying down. The sky was blue and the wind flattened the grass in places. She was picking petals out of a daisy, saying, "He loves me, he loves me not." When she finished she swatted me on the chin with the head of the flower and said, "He loves me not." The flower left a sticky spot on my chin. "How come you don't love me?" she said, and lifted me over her so I felt like I was flying. "Don't you love me?"

"Yes," I said. I thought she was the world.

ANGELS

Three years after I'd finished high school my mother heard from Jolene. I was living outside Philadelphia at the time, renting two rooms over a garage that belonged to a friend of my mother's and selling shirts at a department store on the Main Line called Seal and Cahn. It was Thanksgiving when I found out. My mother and I were alone most of that weekend at her new house in Enfield, eating a lot—acting like we'd always taken this much pleasure eating, and given it as much of our attention. Really, there was nothing else to do. We drifted in and out of the present, never bothering to connect the things we said with anything that really mattered. There were just a lot of people's names and little pieces of news about them to float back and forth at each other.

It was the day after Thanksgiving when she told me. We were in the living room, waiting for more food to heat up for our lunch, reading and talking. I had just finished describing something for her about my job at the store—

telling her that the older men preferred bright colors and coarse fabrics, while the younger men wanted the fluffy shirts with muted tones. It was something I'd seen often, and I thought it might stand as an indication of bigger differences in the generations. "Amazing, isn't it, the kind of things you're forced to speculate about when you sell fifty shirts a day."

"You love that job," she said.

"No, I don't." Now I had a picture of the sales floor and the dark blue carpet and circular racks of coats and pants arranged by size. One thing I'd noticed, no matter how crowded it was, you never heard the sound of people's feet. There were other sounds—voices, music, clothes hangers squeaking on the racks, and the beep of cash registers. Often, coming back out at night I'd have the odd feeling of my senses being turned back on. I'd stand next to my car and listen to things, breathing in air that was not exactly seventy-five degrees with scents of perfume and new cloth in it. "It's a job," I said. "You try to find what's interesting about it."

"Charlie, I'm supposed to tell you . . . there's something I'm supposed to tell you about. You remember Jolene?"

"What do you think?" I smelled turkey from the kitchen.

She smiled nervously, then shut her eyes a moment and closed her book on her fingers, shifting to one side and pulling her feet up under her. "She's written me a few letters recently and she wants to know how you are.

No—she wanted me to let you know she was asking about you."

I looked at her and waited for her to continue. She had on a red cardigan with bright brass buttons, blue slacks, and a necklace of thick green stones shaped like chili beans. She was using color in her hair so it was an unnatural shade of brown with orange highlights.

"What does she say?" I asked.

"What doesn't she say is more like it. She's in some trouble." That seemed to give her an idea. "It's nothing for you to mess around with." The buzzer in the kitchen went off just then. "She wanted me to let you know she was asking after you. That's all." Then she got up to check on our food.

I stayed in the living room a moment longer staring at her empty chair, a new green wingback. There were hollows in it where she'd been sitting and the seat cushion was crushed up against the back. Her book, open on the arm, had a picture of a pink convertible speeding through the desert on the cover, and the words *Restless Hearts* in lacy script above that. I tried to picture Jolene and remember the last time I had seen her. What I saw instead was the beach at Old Saybrook on a day when the sun was gone and the wind lifted the sand a few inches off the ground.

"I might as well tell you," she said when I came into the kitchen. "Jolene is in California trying to be a dyke. But it isn't working. Are you surprised?"

I shrugged. "She was like that. I'm not surprised, and I'm not not-surprised."

"That's exactly what I thought you'd say, Mr. Cool Fish."

"I'm a cool fish . . . Where's her letter?" I asked.

"In the garbage. In the garbage, in the dump, where it belongs. Probably burned up weeks ago."

I wondered what could be in it to make her care so much she had to destroy it. "I wish you'd saved it," I said.

"No. You should be happy I didn't."

THAT WEEKEND I began letters to Jolene in my head and never wrote one of them down. I had opening lines and ways of being sure she would read to the end. But I knew if I tried to write them down I'd only see how unnecessary it was for me to say anything, or for her to listen. That, or I'd realize how impossible it was, after five years of not knowing each other, to see what was important to tell her and what wasn't.

I was taking a course in human development at a college on the Main Line then, to see whether or not I liked it, and whether or not I should consider going to school full-time. We were at a section in the course that had to do with morality and conscience. Just before break our teacher had informed us that, in his opinion, traditional morality was a crock. Most so-called morally advanced people were like cats, he said. They knew right from wrong, but they had no real regard for either. Every law was a broken law, he said, pounding a piece of chalk into his hand, and every action was a self-serving action. That was the truth, and anyone who wasn't willing to see it would never be an honestly moral person. He was emphatic, though he said we shouldn't throw rocks at one another, either. It was a matter of living with what he called the principles of "rigorous personal anarchy."

I'd heard about this lecture from other students before I signed up for the class. It was "Doug's famous lecture." During the sixties and early seventies, students and other professors had crowded the auditorium to hear it. Now there were only the usual faces—the people up in the back sleeping with their coats on or just looking restless, the people in front scribbling things Doug said in their notebooks, though he had said not to worry about that and to just listen. The book I was supposed to read that weekend was his book, but I never read more than the first few sections. I was too distracted thinking about Jolene.

Saturday I spent the afternoon searching the house for anything of Jolene's that had survived the move from my mother's old house, but there was nothing. My mother was at work most of that day. Her room had new light blue miniblinds in the windows and gray carpeting. It was an overcast day and the blinds were half-lowered so the light turned the same dull, grayish blue as the carpet. The room was immaculate and icy, I thought, like no one really lived in it. There were few things there and nothing out of place—lamp, dresser, nightstand, and desk. I could imagine sleeping well in that bed and waking up with no recollection of anything I'd dreamed. My mother had a boyfriend then, Tom. That week Tom was gone, away in Colorado with his kids from his first marriage. He owned two shoe stores. I had never met him, but a few times I'd called and gotten his voice instead of hers at the other end of the line. It was a quiet voice that made me think of a man with thick, dark chest hair and a patient face. I tried to imagine them together in that room, him sitting at the end of the bed in just an under-shirt maybe, stretching his toes or telling her things that had happened to him during his day at work.

I found pictures of Jolene in my mother's desk, along with bills, old bank statements, and other pictures—of me, or my grandmother, and friends of my mother's. The pictures of Jolene were mostly at the beach and in our backyard—Jolene squinting at the sun and waving. Sometimes there would be a drink in her hand, or she would be lying down. There was the day we all went looking for an end table for Jolene, and she wound up buying a foldaway couch instead. There were pictures of the man in charge of delivering the couch standing next to it on the sidewalk, then upstairs in her apartment in the bad light that made him look as if he were in a fish-bowl. They had thought that man was terribly funny. And I remembered a feeling I'd had then that they were using him unfairly—his Greek accent and his over-seriousness about furniture care—for a good laugh, when all along he had thought he was working his charms and about to get a date, or at least make a couple of new friends. Then there was the bed unfolded with the two of them on it, their feet kicked up on pillows, leaning shoulder to shoulder and laughing. I'd taken that one and it was out of focus. I had a shiver of the old aggravation and boredom I used to feel being around them all the time and left out: the way they liked things, which was so intense they rarely seemed to notice how other people didn't care.

"I'LL TELL you what else Jolene told me," my mother said. We were on the way to the train station in Hartford, where I would get a train to New York, then another one to Philadelphia. It was cold and raining lightly, and my mother had her window open a crack so she could smoke a cigarette. "She's going to have her tubes tied."

"That makes sense," I said.

"What are you talking about? It doesn't make any sense at all. Why would she want her tubes tied?"

"She doesn't want kids."

She dragged on her cigarette. "It's an irreversible procedure, Charlie," she said. "Anyway, unless I'm terribly mistaken, women can't have kids with other women." She smiled with part of her mouth.

I shrugged. "Okay, she wants to purge herself," I said, and I laughed. "Get rid of her sexuality. Maybe she'll have a sex change."

"You think you're pretty smart." She looked mad, though she was still smiling. She exhaled and squeezed her cigarette through the crack, then rolled up the window. She went on without looking at me. "Jolene's problem has always been being too much in love with herself, not the opposite. There isn't an ounce of self-destruction in that woman. She wouldn't do a thing to hurt her precious self." She turned the dial on the heat all the way to red. I saw how this talk and the anger just underneath it had as much to do with my going away again as anything else. I wished there was something I could do to make her feel better, but I also knew it wasn't my problem at all.

"Jolene thinks the world is full of favors for her," she said. "Well, I've got news. It isn't."

"She won't do it, you know. Don't worry. She'll talk about it, but it won't ever happen."

"Who's worrying?" she asked.

Before getting out of the car at the station, I told my mother some of the things I had been thinking about her and Jolene, and how it seemed to me that she should overlook any little differences they had rather than lose her as a friend. As I got out of the car I said, "Think about it. Say you'll call her, write her, something."

"It's none of your business what I do."

"You won't be able to live with yourself later on if you don't," I said.

"I can hardly do that as is."

I stood up straight, then leaned back into the car. "I'm going to miss the train," I said. "Could you pop the trunk?"

"Charlie, I appreciate what you're saying, but most things do have to come to an end, you know," she said.

"I know that. I know. Just think about it, okay?"

"You think I haven't been thinking?"

THAT WEEK, while I was at work, I bought two things for Jolene. People were coming into Seal and Cahn more and more for their Christmas shopping, and it put me in a kind of mood where I had to buy something for someone. On my lunch break I went into the women's department and bought her the first two items that caught my attention—a red nightshirt and an angora bomber hat with earflaps. I didn't know how or when I would give her these gifts, but I thought at the moment it mattered less than the impulse to buy them.

The woman who rang up my purchase had been hired at the same time I was. I had seen her during our training, then in the snack bar alone sometimes, or across the parking lot at a deli where many employees took their lunch break. We had never really spoken to each other. I thought she was pretty in a predictable way, medium height and weight, dark, styled hair, and an expression on her face that showed how much she enjoyed the things that were in her control. She wore heavy makeup and dressed carefully in solid colors and tight pants and skirts that fit her well. Often I had stared at her for long moments knowing she would never look up or anticipate my stare. Sometimes I thought she represented everything I never wanted—everything that came with the life of being a salesperson. Other times I wasn't sure what I thought of her except that it was easy to forget what I was doing and stare at her without meaning to.

"Someone special?" she asked as she was ringing up the items.

I nodded.

"*You're* getting a jump on your shopping. I sure don't know when in the world I'm going to find time."

"Why not right now?"

She smiled. "I'm working. Can't you tell?"

"Gosh, sorry." I pretended to be upset with myself for overlooking this. She laughed. "Tonight," I said. "What are you doing tonight?"

She slipped the hat and nightshirt into a light purple plastic bag, and appeared to be thinking. On the bag was the Seal and Cahn logo: a hunter's horn curled around the store name, with the motto "Quality clothes for the gentleman since 1884" underneath.

"I don't know . . . I suppose I could do that," she said. She looked down at the bag again, and cocked her head to one side. I saw she was blushing under all her makeup and trying to figure out what was going on, whether I was coming on to her, or just making a joke.

"I'm off at six," I said.

"Same here."

"Good, where should we meet?" I asked. "Here? We'll get a bite and hit the shops? By the way, my name's Charlie."

"I know," she said. "I remember." We shook hands. Her skin was cold and pale. I noticed that her knuckles and the bones in her fingers were almost as thick as mine, which was surprising since the rest of her was so slight. "Mine's Angel," she said. "See you at six."

THAT NIGHT I watched Angel spend close to a thousand dollars shopping. I had never seen anyone spend this much at one time on gifts. There was no one for me to buy anything for but my mother. I bought her a Dustbuster in the hardware store where Angel bought three coffeemakers for friends, and pruning shears for her father. She bought sheets for her twin sisters at Macy's, travel clocks for her friends at work, four bow ties for her brother. At a boutique in Ardmore called Silky You she tried on three different nightgowns. She called me into the changing room to see each one and give her my opinion: which one would be best for her mother. None were very revealing. I told her to buy the one that looked like an ordinary slip. I thought it hid exactly as much as it revealed without looking like it meant to do either, and it had nice, dark red tones to compliment her skin, which I assumed must be similar to her mother's. I didn't say any of this, though. What I told her was it looked right and she should buy it. That cost almost one hundred dollars by itself.

We were in the changing room together and she was turning circles in front of the mirror, talking about her mother's new husband, and how they'd never gotten to have a real honeymoon. I wondered if her knees were naturally that knocked together, or if she was doing something to hold herself this way because she knew I was looking and the gown stopped several inches above her knees. "Don't stare," she said. She looked back at my reflection over her shoulder. "It's just like a bathing suit. You don't stare at girls on the beach, do you."

"Hah," I said. "That is nothing like a bathing suit." I cleared my throat. "I'll be out here waiting," I said, and I went back out on the sales floor to sit between mannequins and packages of underwear and stockings, waiting for her and feeling a little overwhelmed by everything.

At her apartment we sat on the floor on a thick fake-fur rug that was almost as soft as a bed. "The cat loves it," she told me and curled up like she wished she were a cat herself, across from me with her back against the couch, balancing a glass of white wine on her knee.

"Where does all this money come from?" I asked. Her apartment was nice, not lavish, the furniture all solid wood and permanent-seeming: white bookshelves, an oak end table, matching gray lamps at either end of the couch, plants hanging from the ceiling.

"I save. Ever since I was a little girl, I save. All year, fifty dollars out of the paycheck—at least—right in my Christmas fund, just like that," she said, inserting something into an imaginary piggybank. "I don't even think about it. Everyone knows at Christmas I'm the world's biggest spender." She paused. "What about you?"

"I hate Christmas. I've hated it as long as I can remember." I thought about the Dustbuster I'd bought for my mother, and felt a fleeting embarrassment. I wondered why I'd bought it and what she would think—whether she would be able to make it mean something more than it did. Probably she would. "It's a giant feeding frenzy in the name of a baby nobody cared about until after he was dead."

"What an awful thing to say."

"It's the truth. And he wouldn't approve of it any more than I do."

"How do you know?"

"I just do."

All the rest of that night there was conflict and disagreement in the things we talked about. Still, we never stopped laughing at each other. I had to ask her a few times why I was there. I would stare, smile back at her thin, chalky face and say, "We have absolutely nothing in common. Music, taste, jokes, movies—what are we doing?"

"There must be things," she said. "We just haven't found them yet. Who did you buy the hat for? Me?"

"An old friend," I said. "You, I hardly know."

"Oh. Girlfriend or just friend?"

I shrugged.

"Come on, Charlie, she's your old girlfriend, isn't she," she said. "There. Case in point: you wouldn't be thinking of her at all if it wasn't Christmas, right? That's a good thing, isn't it, to be thinking about someone you care about?"

"It is," I conceded.

"Christmases make you think about the people you love, remember why you love them, and buy them a gift." She pulled on her fingers as she made these points, like she needed to count them for me. "That's what's good about it."

"I think it's disgusting."

"Then you're disgusting. Where's your girlfriend now?"

"I don't know."

"What do you mean, you don't know? How are you going to give her that present you bought? Are you going to see her?"

I shook my head. "I haven't seen her in about five years."

"You haven't seen her, even once?"

I shook my head.

"That's so sweet you bought her something and you don't know where she is." She paused and then leaned forward with her chin in her hands, studying me. "How are you going to find her?"

"Directory assistance," I said. "I don't know. She's somewhere in San Francisco."

"You two are still in love, aren't you?"

"It has nothing to do with love. I just wanted to buy her something."

"God, that's so nice," she said.

I reached out and ran a finger down her face, from her forehead to her lips. It was surprising that I didn't feel any of her makeup coming off on my finger, though I could see it shining dully all over her skin. She closed her eyes. "Why do you think that's so nice?" I asked.

She opened her eyes again. "I just think it isn't very often when people are that much in love and they should let each other know."

"I never said anything about love." I put my hand on her shoulder and then moved it up the back of her neck, under her hair.

"Oh no," she said. She patted me roughly on the leg. Then, when I didn't let go of her she leaned over to kiss my cheek and I heard something flutter in my eardrum, some pressure releasing as she came closer—her temperature and all the sharp perfumey fragrances covering her. I flinched just as her lips touched me. She sat back on her knees, waiting for something I didn't know about. She wiggled slightly so her hair went straight back over her shoulders. I thought about some of the magazine pictures and TV ads I'd seen of women who looked like that—cute, sexy, deodorized things. And I wondered if those ideas were really Angel's and the pictures helped them to take form, or if it happened the other way around.

"Why did you jump like that?" she asked.

"An allergic reaction to your cosmetics, I think. You smell like my grandmother." I sniffed for effect and wiped my nose.

"Baloney. I'm not good enough. You jumped because I'm not good enough." She paused, then went on in a lighter tone to soften the attack on herself—and I knew I was meant to understand the attack had come from me indirectly. "Your heart's already given to someone else," she said. "She's your perfect match."

I shook my head. "You're crazy."

"I am not," she said. She stood up and walked out of the room, weaving slightly, and went into the bathroom, where she left the door half-open so I could hear her running water into the sink. "See you tomorrow," she said. "That front door locks by itself."

THE DAY after shopping with Angel I called my mother to find out Jolene's address. I'd just gotten off work. "Charlie, I really don't want you meddling in any of this," she said. "I will call Jolene when I'm good and ready."

"I'm not meddling. I just wanted to drop her a note. Nothing to do with you. So where is she?"

I heard something jostle on the other end of the phone, then she was blowing her nose. "I don't remember. It's something-Geary Street, number eleven. You want me to find it?"

"That's why I called."

"Well, I don't know where it is. You'll have to give me a second." She dropped the phone, then a few minutes later picked up somewhere else in the house. "I have no idea what I did with that address," she said. "I honestly don't, but here's her phone number."

"Thanks," I said. "I was just going to send her a note."

"Well, you'll have to call first," she said, and gave me the number. "It should be right. I really don't want you interfering in anything that isn't your business."

"I won't."

"Anything else new?"

"No," I said, and waited a moment. "No," I said again, because there was nothing else to say to her.

"Good. You talk to Jolene and tell her I send my best."

"I will."

ANGEL WANTED to know more about Jolene. We were at the deli across from Seal and Cahn, watching shoppers come in and out of the big glass doors of the store. I'd had a turkey sandwich and a glass of water. Angel was still nibbling a diet salad that looked like it was mostly parsley and bean sprouts. There was some cranberry-tinted ice left in the glass next to her plate.

I said I was never very interested in another person's past. To me it was like a confusing silent movie whenever someone started telling me his life story—endless details going nowhere. "You'll just get bored," I said.

"Not me," she said. She rattled the ice in her glass, then tilted it back to get the last of what was melted at the bottom, her breath steaming the inside white, and set it back on the table. She looked at me. "Really," she said. "Tell it."

"There was this big age difference problem with Jolene. That was what it boiled down to."

"Why are you starting at the end?" She chewed some ice. "I want the whole thing."

"It was the same at the beginning as it was at the end," I said.

"How profound."

"Nothing profound about it," I said.

"So, essentially nothing happened—you're saying?"

"No, I never said that." I told her what I could. I said my impression now was that I had been sick the whole time—sick, and outside of things, but in love with it all too. I used the word "delirious" too many times. "It was just . . . it was like we were freaks. Like it was a sickness."

"I can see that," she said, and looked away.

I leaned toward her with my elbows on the table and smiled. "I told you it was boring."

"It's not boring at all. It's upsetting. Didn't you ever stop and think, you know, maybe this isn't such a great idea—maybe I should get help? What if I get her pregnant? Then what? I can see it now."

"I don't know," I said. "I was young. I didn't get her pregnant."

"*That's* good," she said, with an emphasis I thought I wasn't meant to understand.

I shrugged.

She told me about a friend she'd had in junior high. The girl's name was Rhona and she had liked to make up stories about perverse things that happened to her in the woods of Maine, where she spent her summers. Angel was sure most of what Rhona said never happened, though at the time that didn't make it any less impressive to hear about. "I mean, just the fact she could think of these things," she pointed at her head, "it was crazy enough."

"Yes." I glanced at my watch and saw we were already five minutes late getting back to work. "So, what happened?" I asked. "Is Rhona the one that got pregnant?"

"No." Angel looked at me and then away, as if I'd led her somewhere slightly confusing. She glanced down at her hands a moment, took a breath, and appeared to remember what she was going to say. "Nothing happened. We stopped being friends, drifted apart, different groups. You know, that thing when you reach a certain age, and you start to develop, and your personality, your tastes and everything come out. Then, suddenly you realize there are these people you can't stand. Half the people in the world, actually—you have nothing in common with, you can't stand them."

"Like me," I said.

"I never said I couldn't stand you!"

I knew I had forced her into this, but I hadn't expected she would correct me with so much conviction. She grabbed my hand across the table and squeezed it. Her hand was cold on mine. She had a puzzle ring on her middle finger and thin, turquoise and silver bands around her other fingers. "I'm so sorry," she said. "I didn't mean to sound like that. Really, I didn't, Charlie. I like you. I really like you."

"It's okay," I said.

She released my hand and leaned to one side. "It's not your fault, what happened with Jolene. You were just a kid. She's the one who should have known better."

I nodded and leaned over too, took some of her salad and put it in my mouth. I thought her irises were the same bright, frayed green as the parsley I was mashing between my front teeth and for a moment the two were one thing in my mind—her eyes and the parsley. And I wondered if I would always have to think of the taste of parsley when I looked closely at her eyes, or the other way around. "We're late," I said. She looked at her watch, and suddenly we were running back across the parking lot.

WE HAD lunch together every day that week. Angel liked best of all to speculate about Jolene and invent theories explaining what she must be doing with her life and why. If there was any one thing that held us there at the little tile-top table next to the front window of the deli where we always ate, Jolene was it. We would drift around from one topic to another, picking up minor points and dropping them—how much time off her boss had compared with mine, or why the people in small leather goods were so stuck up, and what was the latest gossip about the shared bathroom issue. Then one of us would mention something about Jolene and suddenly there were no gaps in the things we said to each other. At times I was fairly sure talking about her was just a way for us to think out loud about ourselves; other times I couldn't say what in the world was going on, though I had the feeling Angel thought she was helping me to figure out something important.

In the end, Jolene was anything we made her. I was

always trying to steer the conversation back to us, but all Angel ever wanted was to make up things about Jolene. She was married and divorced, twice, to a millionaire art dealer who was always hiring people to paint and sculpt her. She'd gone to California in 1979 to remake herself. Now she lived alone in an inexpensive, down-home kind of apartment in the Haight district and worked at a Planned Parenthood office in another part of town. She didn't work because she needed the money—she got plenty from her ex. She wanted redemption. She wanted things stripped down, back to basics, so she could really feel what most affected her, and work at something she thought mattered: birth control. And she hated men because of everything she knew about them, though there was also this lingering connection, the private struggle for control that she would have to play out every day in her work.

"Here's the main thing, Charlie," she would say. "Jolene's just one of these people who's never going to be satisfied in life. You know that—that's what you're up against here: someone who's never satisfied. Who knows? It could even be chemical." This was often the final point she would arrive at. "That's probably it. She's one of them," she said.

"No. That doesn't sound right to me," I said. "Too easy."

"Of course. That's why you have to see her again—to get the real information firsthand."

"I never said I had to see her again."

"Of course you do. You're just stuck in this little groove until you take care of her."

"No. No I'm not," I said, but I knew opposing her on a point like this was nearly the same thing as admitting she was right.

"Sure," she said, and pushed her cheek out with her tongue, trying not to laugh.

A few more days and we started to talk about quitting our jobs and driving across the country together, making it back for Christmas. We still had three and a half weeks. We talked, but the talk wasn't very real. We could see Jolene, give her the present, and leave. I don't remember who started it, but the idea possessed us quickly. We would lose a lot of money being out of work the best time of the year, but that was okay. We could help each other and get new jobs.

Back in the store I was feeling more and more like a person who could see through walls. Once I let a man have a shirt for free, without telling him. I just put it in the bag with the other things he'd bought and never rang it up. Another man came in looking for a rugby shirt and I told him not to buy one. I said our rugby shirts were stupidly designed and overpriced. They'd be out of style in another year anyway. He should buy himself a tie instead. Then, when I heard two customers quietly discussing the price of a corduroy jacket I told them that everything in the store had a certain value only if you believed it did, and if you wanted something, you should just get it. I said value was too petty to let it ruin your life by arguing, trying to outguess the future and know ahead of time what style would last and what price was the best bargain. These things were all predetermined anyway, by fashion people we would never know or see.

One of them asked if I was on commission to philosophize, or not, and I said I was. That wasn't the point. The point was living the right kind of life. "So, maybe you save twenty dollars at Penney's or Ward's. Maybe you save ten. I doubt you save ten. But did you like that jacket as much as you liked this one? And in a few years, what matters more, the jacket or the ten dollars?" They put the jacket on a credit card and walked out of the store, starry-eyed.

The day before Angel and I left for California, on my way home from work, I was suddenly more depressed than I'd been in a long time. I didn't know, then, that we would be going to California the next day, and I suppose it might have made a difference if I had. I was at a traffic light on Lancaster, stopped between a Jaguar and a Mercedes, looking at the gray sky that was the same blank color as the road and all the bare trees, and I was thinking about my life. I thought that nothing was turning out like I'd imagined. Nothing in the store where I worked mattered to me. And I tried to think of something that did matter, but there was nothing—only those two slick, glassy cars that were not mine, though I wanted them, one stopped behind me and the other in front of me.

I went forward as the light turned green, and tried not to think at all. This was easy since it was my regular mode for driving home at the end of the day—turn on the radio and don't think. "This is my life," I said, "and it is not very interesting."

When I got home, I called Angel. We talked awhile and I told her I was sick of my life.

"So, get a new one," she said.

Later in the conversation we ended up convincing each other that tomorrow was the day. We would meet at the end of my driveway at dawn with all the money we could spare, beat the early traffic, and go to California.

THAT NIGHT I hardly slept at all. It was windy and the wind ran right through the wall I slept next to. I moved my bed into the middle of the room, where it had been all the winter before, and piled everything I owned on top of it to stay warm. There were blankets and shirts and jackets everywhere—discontinued things I had gotten for cheap at Seal and Cahn. I had an old milk-house heater that my landlady, Mrs. Garcia, had given me to use when I first moved in, but it didn't do much unless you stood directly in front of it.

At about two o'clock I realized it was only eleven

o'clock in California and I decided now was the time, if ever, to call Jolene and tell her what I was planning. I thought there was nothing so surprising about my decision to do this. It was probably the thing keeping me from falling asleep in the first place—it just had to be done if Angel and I were really going to leave in the morning. I put on another pair of pants over the sweatpants I had on, a shirt, and a sweatshirt, and went into the kitchen. I dialed her number and waited. I was staring at the floor, one corner where the brown paint had been stripped away and there was an indentation that looked as if it had been left by something heavy that sat for a long time—a radiator, I thought—when she answered.

"Jolene," I said. "It's me."

"Me who?" she said.

"Me. Charlie." There was a sound like something had fallen onto the floor.

"Just a sec," she said. Then a moment later, "Charlie—as in Mary and Charlie. My god, isn't this a surprise!" She sounded out of breath. "How are you?" she asked. I heard a man in the background yelling something at her about where to hang the penguins. Another person was imitating Jolene, saying, "Mary and Charlie—it's Charlie, as in Mary and Charlie."

"I'm all right," I said. "Doing all right. I wanted to tell you, a friend of mine and I are driving out to California tomorrow."

"You're what? Hang on a second. Sorry." I heard her hand rubbing against the mouthpiece, then she yelled something and a door banged shut. "There. Now I can hear. I'm in the bathroom. There's a little party here, decorating the tree. Charlie, I've missed you a lot—what is this? What are you saying about California?"

"That's right, tomorrow." As I spoke I realized I was still staring into that corner where the paint was stripped and the floor was depressed, and when I realized this it also occurred to me that I hadn't really been seeing it at all. I looked around the room. There were dishes in the sink, and a package of cheese was out on the counter with cheese crumbs around it and a knife stuck in it. This had to do with my dinner. "You'd hate the place where I live," I said. "It's a real hole."

"Wait a minute, wait a minute. When are you coming?" She sounded slightly drunk, the way she was rushing her words.

"Tomorrow. It's kind of all of a sudden, I guess, but that's just the way it is."

"How long can you stay?"

"That's not definite. Depends how long it takes us."

"Charlie, are you all right? What's going on?"

"I'm fine."

"You want to know if you can have a place to stay with your friend. Is that it?" she asked. "The answer is, of course. You're always welcome here."

"Good," I said.

"Tell me—tell me all about yourself. What are you doing? Are you in college now? Your mother said something that you were going to take a class—some classes."

"I'll tell you all that when we get there. I can't really talk. I haven't gotten anything together for the trip yet."

"Okay. This is a wonderful surprise, Charlie," she said. "Really, really wonderful. Be sure and call right away when you get here. I really have missed you. Don't disappoint me, now, my hopes are up."

"I'll try," I said.

"What's your friend's name—so I can tell my housemates. In case one of you calls when I'm out."

"Angel," I said. "Angel Landino. Italian, I guess."

"You're kidding! We'll have two Angels then: mine and yours."

"What are you talking about?"

"My girlfriend's Angel, too—at least, before, she was—Angelica Reilly." She ran the names together unsurely, like she was just letting her tongue find whatever name-sounds would roll off it. "I mean, we still see each other. She doesn't live here, but you'll meet her eventually."

"Great," I said.

"Heavenly, to be more to the point." She laughed. "This will be wonderful, all these people from the past . . . Hal Gold, you probably don't remember him. He just appeared in town the other day. Unbelievable, unbeliev-able, but there he was."

"Okay," I said, to save her from stumbling on any fur-ther. "Now I really have to go. I'll call again sometime when we're closer."

"Call collect," she said. "I'm writing it down now so everyone here knows: collect from Charlie or Angel Lando-linguine—whatever it was—yes. Big yes. This is really, really a wonderful suprise, Charlie. I'm so glad you're doing this!"

"I'm glad you're so glad," I said, and we hung up shortly after that. I meant to clean the place a little before I left, but I never did. I went back to bed in a kind of trance, and fell immediately to sleep. I dreamed about myself as a fat little baby sitting in a cloud with my eyes closed. I had fake, gold-lacquered hair and a plastic harp covered with frost in my lap. I kept thinking what a foolish idea it was for me to be sitting there in a cloud with a plastic harp, asleep, but there I was, and my eyes wouldn't open no matter how hard I tried to make them.

ANGEL WOKE me, banging at my door. I felt like I'd slept years in those few hours, and I could have slept years more. She looked around and said she thought she would probably be warmer waiting for me in the car, and I agreed, though I thought she looked unwilling to wait at all. I could see how little it might take to make her change her mind, go home, go back to sleep, and forget the whole thing.

I found my overnight bag in the closet. It still had some of the clothes I'd brought with me to my mother's two weeks ago. I piled more clothes on top of that— threw in a sweater and the block of cheese with the knife in it from the kitchen last of all. We could eat that. Then I changed what I had on, and ran downstairs. Angel was in the passenger seat with her coat on and her eyes closed. Her car was a light blue Rabbit. It was running, sputtering quietly, and frost was melting off the top. I took one last look around at the yard, the big dim shape of the Garcias' house in the mist behind it, and got in next to Angel. The clock on her dashboard said it was just after six o'clock as I backed out of the driveway.

"Tell me we aren't really doing this," she said, without opening her eyes.

"We aren't doing anything."

"If I was awake enough I'd stop you right now before we got anywhere," she said.

"Shh," I said. "Sleep."

"Am I stupid, or what? Why don't we take your car?"

"The old bomb."

"Am I crazy?"

I didn't answer at first. We passed under a street lamp and in the pink light I saw her hair was down, uncombed and coming away from her forehead in loose dark swirls where she usually combed it or tied it straight back. Her face without makeup was startlingly white, like someone had a flashlight under her chin. "No. You're beautiful," I said.

She faced me and opened her eyes. "I am *not*. I'm as plain as sin, and you know it."

Her mouth was smaller than I had thought. There was a curve in her lower lip that made it stick out. "Then you obviously don't know the first thing about yourself," I said.

"And neither do you," she said. She turned away, sucking on her lip. Soon she closed her eyes again. She slept most of the morning. We were well across the state of Pennsylvania before she woke up. She asked if I'd remembered Jolene's gift. We were at a rest area and she had just finished making herself up in the bathroom. I told her I had, but in fact it was still in the backseat of my car at home, forgotten.

That whole first day was a blur of sleeping and fighting sleep, trading driving off and on. We barely spoke. Radio stations came and went. We made it over the Ohio border where we stopped for an early dinner—roasted chicken at a Best Western restaurant—and drove on.

."Do you want to know why I'm doing this?" she asked, just after dark. "I can tell you, now I've had some time to think about it."

There were often these odd lags in our conversation

that day, where one or both of us would seem to have forgotten what was happening. "Yes. Why?" I said, when I realized she was waiting for me to say something.

"Because it's the kind of thing that in ten years I'm going to wish I did, but then it'll be too late. Now it's not too late."

"I like that," I said, and waited, but she didn't have anything to add.

She drove the last part of the night while I slept. I barely remember parking in front of a motel room and checking in—seeing a lot of Indiana plates. Then I fell asleep again on a crooked fold-out bed, watching the bathroom door across the room from me, the light coming around it, and waiting for her to be finished so I could go wash my hands and brush my teeth before I slept. When I woke up it was dark in the room and Angel was snoring lightly. I went and stood over her awhile, watching her sleep. I held my hand over her face to feel her breath come and go. Then I took off my clothes and got in bed next to her. I was careful to lift the sheets without uncovering her, and never let any part of myself touch her. When I woke up again she was still snoring, and the early light was like milk. Her arm had fallen across my neck. I got up, kissed her once where her lower lip was thickest, then went back into the fold-out bed and lay there waiting for her to wake up.

ANGEL TALKED about herself most of the next day. She told me about her family—her twin sisters, Debra and Marcie. They were two years older than she, four years older than her brother, Kevin. Both sisters had gone to Ivy League universities, majored in science, raced each other in sprints, and competed on the high dive. Angel couldn't say which of them was better at any of the things they did, partly because she had been raised to believe comparing them was wrong and would bring disastrous consequences, partly because they were, in fact, always so dead even. They were identical. She said she used to watch them sometimes sitting together at church and singing when they were all much younger. It was eerie, she said. Their mouths moved in exactly the same way. They had the same expression on their faces. They would even forget or stumble over words at the same time, and they did this without ever looking at each other. The only real difference between them was their hair, she said. It was the same brown-blond color, but Debra's hair was duller than Marcie's because she never took care of it. Eventually it got dried out and lost its sheen. This was how most people could tell them apart.

"They were famous, you know. Everything they did, they did it the best. They used to trade boyfriends back and forth just so they could dump them and make them look bad. One guy—his name was Dennis—Marcie got him alone one night. Of course, Debra's hiding right under her bed. They have this all planned out because Debra and Dennis just broke up, and he thinks Debra is gone for the weekend. Anyway, Marcie and Dennis are going at it and Marcie says, 'Dennis, tell me, is this how Debra does it?' or something like that. She gets him talking about Debra, what it's like doing it with her and so on. Then, of course, Debra gets out from under the bed and they skewer the poor guy."

"That's unbelievable," I said.

"Of course it is. That's how they were. Do you have any idea what that's like, though—growing up in the shadow of the famous Haverford twins?"

"No," I said. "I mean, now I do, but I had no idea."

"Princesses," she said. "They were . . . goddamn princesses."

We were in Indiana and Illinois for most of that day, and everything I saw out the window had something to do with Angel's twin sisters: there were matching corn-fields to either side of us full of imaginary twins doing back walkovers and drinking soda upside down, and in all the cars coming back at us on the eastbound strip of freeway, twins were sitting there talking about their boyfriends. I wondered if there was something I had done or something about me that was making Angel think so much about her sisters, or if they were just continually on her mind.

"There were two of them, and they were the freaks, but

I was alone. Do you know what that's like? Growing up with a couple of freak overachievers who keep telling you that you're weird because you're so normal?" she said. "I'm normal."

"Hard for you to formulate your own idea of yourself," I said. "That must have been hard."

"Spare me the psychology. I forgot you were taking that class."

"It's human development, not psychology. There's a difference."

"What's that?"

I didn't answer right away, because I didn't have an answer. "We haven't covered that yet. It's got something to do with education."

She laughed. "That's what I like about you."

"What?"

"That you never pay attention unless you feel like it."

We stopped for gas and while Angel was filling up I went inside to pay, buy gum for her, and get a bag of pop-corn to eat. We were just past the Indiana-Illinois border then. The man behind the counter was listening to Chris-tian music and grinning fiercely at customers like he was a cartoon. He was very fat and he had his arms propped up on his belly. His hands moved at the wrists as he counted my change, flicking it across the counter at me. "Bless you and have a nice day," he said, and flashed me the cartoon smile.

Getting back in the car I noticed it smelled distinctly like Angel and me—the combination of our clothes, our breath, and the hotel soap we used.

She opened the gum, took a stick, and offered me one. "I was just listening. There's supposed to be a storm tonight," she said, switching off the radio.

"Big one?" I asked. I wanted to say something about that fat man at the register inside, just to make her laugh. That was the difference in the way I was seeing things now—I was always thinking about her and ways to repeat what I'd seen for her so she would laugh.

"There's a winter storm watch. Snow, then sleet and rain, back to snow again. I don't think we'll be going anywhere tomorrow," she said.

"Great. Let's make it to Iowa City, at least."

"At least," she said.

The rest of that day she finished telling me about her twin sisters. They had married twin brothers, Bill and Zane, and no one in the family was happy with this. I was watching her out of the corner of my eye while I drove and she talked. I could see just her legs without turning to face her—her thighs on the vinyl seat. She had on blue jeans that were faded almost white, except around her fly, where it was darker and the orange threads showed. I couldn't keep my eyes from that. I wanted to hold her around the legs and sink my face into her. I could imagine every detail of it. I thought she must know my thoughts somehow, or feel them, but there was no way to tell and no indication she was thinking anything like what I was.

Just before dark we got in a ridiculous, half-serious argument about the right way to make change for a customer—bills or coins first, change on the counter or right in the hand. I said it didn't much matter because the point of sale was already passed: make your change quickly and get to the next customer, I said. Sell, sell, sell. Angel disagreed. She said customers were actually the most sensitive at the purchase point, and it would be a real violation of their trust if you didn't handle them and their money carefully—as carefully as you handled the merchandise. Smile a lot, she said. Selling goes on all the way until they're out the door, she said. I held out my hand for her to demonstrate, and she counted some imaginary change into it while I grabbed at the tips of her fingers.

"See how sensitive you are," she said. "You want to know I'm giving you back exactly as much as you get. Grabby, grabby!" She laughed.

"That's why I keep it out on the counter. No one's feelings get hurt that way," I said. "Here's your change."

"That's impossible. Feelings are always hurt or you wouldn't have any."

"It's their problem then. People should be able to look after themselves," I said.

"Hard ass. No wonder you sell less than anyone else in shirts."

"Like hell! Who says?"

She was holding my hand, counting more imaginary money into it. "I have my sources. Four seventy-five, five, and ten," she said. "Now, wouldn't you come back for more?"

"I would. Of course I would." I leaned out of my seat then, closer to her.

"Just think, they're all back there now, getting ready to go home . . . "

"I'm going to kiss you," I said, "so we know what it's like." Her mouth fit almost inside mine. She sucked my lower lip between her teeth while she made a humming noise in her throat and bit gently, then pushed her tongue along the side of my tongue. For a moment I thought something had jumped on the back of my head, but it was only her hand there.

"Watch the road," she said. I'd veered off into the shoulder and the gravel was rumbling under us.

We were silent a moment after that.

"This is not exactly what I expected," she said coolly. Then she was laughing. "Oh, I don't know what I expected. Maybe this is what I expected. Maybe it is. Maybe it isn't." She continued to laugh, then put her hand on the back of my neck and squeezed. "You," she said. "You know, you have one of the nicest voices."

"I do?"

"Yes. I have a thing about voices. Before, when I was young, if I heard a person talk—certain people—I'd get this urge to chew on something. Seriously!" She clenched her teeth and made a noise in the back of her throat. "I'd have to put something in my mouth and chew on it. I had this rubber keychain I took around with me most of the time. Actually, there were toothmarks on everything I owned. And then sometimes I'd hear a voice that made me want to stroke the inside of my wrist, or my forearms— mostly men's voices, that were warm and rich." She touched my cheek, then began tracing patternless designs with the tips of her fingers on the back of my neck.

"So, what does my voice make you want to do?"

"Nothing. It's just nice. I don't have those impulses anymore," she said. "Only distantly. But I notice voices." There was a silence. "So, tell me something."

"What?"

"Anything, so I can hear you talk. You grew up in Connecticut, right?"

"Yes." Knowing she liked my voice made me worry about talking to her. I wondered whether I'd be able to sound like I always had, or if having this new information about the ways she listened to me would ruin whatever it was I'd been doing naturally all along.

"So, how did you get to Philadelphia?"

"This friend of mine, Jake, from high school. He was a

year ahead of me. So when I graduated—he was at U Penn—he said I should come visit him. I spent about a month and I liked it, so I stayed." I knew I was saying things awkwardly.

"I see." She yawned, then leaned against me with her head on my shoulder. "Mmm," she said. "I'm glad you did. So tell me about Jake. You never said anything about him before."

"Jake. He was like my best friend." I told her about a night toward the end of my time visiting him when he and I walked a mile in the rain, coming home from a movie, and how he refused to share my umbrella because he didn't want to pretend it wasn't raining. "Jake had this thing, like he wanted to feel as if there were nothing between himself and what was real. The more uncomfortable he felt the more he figured he was getting to the heart of reality." I was in the middle of telling her this when I realized she had fallen asleep. "Angel," I said. She didn't answer. I liked the sound of my voice saying her name, and imagined I could hear in it something like the quality she said was nice. "Angel," I said again.

"What?"

"I'm just saying your name."

There was a silence. "This is the longest trip I've ever been on," she said. "You know, it doesn't even feel like a trip anymore, it's just like sitting in a car all day, waiting for the day to be over."

BEFORE ANYTHING else, we counted all our money on the motel bed. She still had seven hundred dollars we hadn't touched; I had five hundred and change. I put most of this in a roll, which she fastened with a hair elastic and stuck in the bag where she kept her cosmetics.

"Safe," she said. "You let me keep track of this, I think we'll be okay. We'll split whatever's left." She snapped the bag shut and put it on the nightstand beside her, patting it once as if to assure us both it was really there. "I just can't believe this place: thirty-eight a night."

"It's nice," I said. The room was all muted rose and beige colors, with a cream-colored carpet and peach and tan striped wallpaper. The bed was a huge square at the center of the room with a window in the wall across from it. "Nice place to be stuck in a blizzard."

"No snow yet," she said. She unfastened her barette, then pulled and straightened her hair so it went over her shoulders, and fell back next to me on her back with her legs hanging off the edge of the bed. She held her arms up like she meant to touch me, then folded them across her chest. There was some stiffness at the corners of her mouth I thought I was supposed to take for a smile. Her eyes moved quickly from place to place, anywhere my eyes weren't. I tried to think of something I could do to set her at ease, or assure her that I was thinking of her in all the ways she might want to be thought of, but I was pretty sure it was impossible. I touched her eye where the stripe of copper paint that covered her eyelid began. "You can wash this off," I said. "Now we're alone and you don't have anyone to impress." I could see the talc and powder, sparkling everywhere on her cheeks, and her lipstick, which was smudged so it looked like she had two mouths, one slightly bigger sitting on top of the other.

"It's hardly anything at all," she said. She closed her eyes for a moment. "A little eye shadow."

I put my hand behind her head and lifted her face to mine, upside down. "I want to see you again—what you look like."

Her eyes were set on something behind me on the ceiling. "Let go, Charlie," she said.

She got up then and went into the bathroom. Her hair was creased and shiny where she'd just undone it, with more red there than elsewhere. "I think we should go out—walk around. Get some exercise." The door was half-open. I watched her douse a cotton ball with something from a frosted bottle and scrub circles with it on her cheeks, then swipe it over her eyes. She leaned over the sink splashing water everywhere. "We just sit in that car all day, it's not healthy. We should go out and walk around or something," she said. She blew water away from her mouth, then scrubbed at her eyes again. "Don't you think?"

"Okay. But let's eat first." On the lower shelf of the nightstand was a flier printed on orange paper describing items available to guests. "Here's something about room service. Wednesday night—says we can have the ziti or fried chicken dinner."

"Wait," she said. She closed the door and a few minutes later came out again. She had on a plain white shirt, which she'd left untucked, the tails wrinkled and standing out around her waist. "I'll call," she said. She sat down next to me and picked up the phone. While she dialed I sat up behind her and pulled her back against my chest. I slid my hands through the buttons in her shirt, pulling a few of the lower ones undone. "Yes," she said. "Room service. We wanted two of those fried chicken dinners." She hadn't rebuttoned the top button of her jeans or closed her belt. I touched the elastic of her underwear, then moved my hands back along her stomach. She put her hand over mine to stop me, then let go. "We're in sixty-eight," she said. "No, we'll pay tomorrow—that's fine." She hung up the phone, turned around, and pushed me back on the bed with her legs between mine. "See?" she said. "Is that better? Now you can see my ugly face. Is that what you want?" She moved away a few inches so I could see her, then moved in close again. Her eyelashes were dark and short, still wet, and the fuzz outlining the hinges of her jaw was also streaked with water. Her whole face was surprisingly and appealingly pale. For a moment I had the weird idea she was someone I'd known all my life and somehow not recognized, or temporarily forgotten. It must have been the effect of seeing her undisguised after so long.

"It's better than anything in the world," I said.

"Oh, not quite," she said.

I sat up, lifting her with me so that her legs went around me. She was twisting to one side to resist the position we were in and she looked a little scared. "I'm not a mirror," I said. "Look at me—look. I don't see what you see when I look at you."

"That's so stupid. I know you're not a mirror." She pinched the sleeve of her shirt where it was quivering like she'd been caught in an invisible breeze. "Look, I'm shaking," she said. I kissed the corners of her mouth where it was still faintly orange from her makeup and lipstick.

"Stop. Just stop it," she said.

"What?"

She didn't answer right away, then she climbed a little higher against me, and pushed my head down into her chest. "Just, slow," she said. "Slow down. It's been so long since I've been like this with anyone." Her shirt smelled like soap and sweat. I could feel how hot her skin was under it, and I heard her heart thumping where my face was squashed against her. She reached in front of me, opened the last few buttons of her shirt, and let it fall off over her shoulders, moving my head where she wanted. "Small, but they're perfect," she said quietly. "Do you think? Perfectly shaped—now I can't believe I just said that." I could see very little to agree or disagree with what she had said. I heard my breath moving over her skin, and felt the heat come back in my face. She tightened her hold of my hair, pulling me away and pushing me down at the same time. "No, don't stop," she said. I felt her swell in my mouth, her skin tightening against my teeth, and there was a metallic taste on my tongue like the smell of her sweat. She let go and swept her hands across my back, then grabbed my hair again.

Later that night we found a tray with our dinners outside the door—matching dishes of withered chicken along with some carrots and rice, big drops of cold condensation left on the inside of the tin plate covers. We ate what we could, but the chicken was salty, like bologna, and the carrots had no taste at all, though they were the brightest orange vegetables I'd ever seen. Afterward, I watched Angel hack apart everything left on our plates, so it would look as if we'd eaten it, then put the whole mess back out in the hall on the tray it had come on, to be taken away.

"That was awful," she said, rubbing her fingers around her mouth to wipe away the last traces. She had put her shirt on again and was still wearing a pair of thick mustard socks that had fallen down around her ankles. Her legs were thinner and smaller than I had imagined or remembered from the night she was trying on lingerie.

And her knees *were* slightly knocked so that it looked like she was kicking something in front of her as she came back across the room to me, pulling the tails of her shirt down around her. "I didn't even hear them ring. Did you?"

"They probably didn't ring. They must have known better," I said.

"That is so embarrassing. I can't believe it."

"Stop saying you can't believe it," I said.

She flopped down next to me on the bed. I moved my arm so she could lie under it with the top of her head touching my side.

"No one knows who we are," I said.

"I know they don't know. I'm not dumb." She paused. "You don't think they really heard, though?" I didn't answer her. She let out a breath and sank back closer. "Jolene," she said scornfully.

"What?"

"Jolene-shmolene. *She* wouldn't care, would she."

"Probably not."

She kicked a leg up straight in front of her. "And how do I know what you'll remember about this ten years from now? You could forget all about it." She let her leg fall back on the bed. "You could get to San Francisco and forget all about it, just like you forgot her present."

"How did you know?"

She rolled over on top of me and sat up. "But you won't forget me," she said. "I'm better than her, any day."

She was being more playful than I had realized. Now she had most of her weight on the heel of one hand, leaning into my chest. It was a pleasant kind of pressure that almost hurt—a pinch going between my muscles to my lungs. She pushed back and took my hands in hers, led them under her shirt, and put them on her hips. "I have the nicest hips. Did you notice?"

"I was about to say something . . ."

She put her fingers, which still smelled like bad chicken, over my mouth and said, "Don't talk. No more talking now."

THE NEXT day we walked around Iowa City waiting for snow, but snow never came. The sky was solid gray and the air felt like it was packed and static with moisture. We walked to the old capitol and then to the river, where ducks sped along a current under the bridge, snatching invisible, edible things out of the cold water and making a racket. We had lunch in a deli like the one across from Seal and Cahn—sandwiches and beer—and, realizing how hungry we were, went to another place where we did it all over again. I had a mild kind of headache from not sleeping most of the night before. Everything was unclear. Some of the individual details in what I saw, though, stood out in ways I didn't expect: the exact slope of the ground and the way it ran into mud at the edge of the river, or the sound of a bird taking off from a bush after we'd startled it. There was a line of small, embryonic pimples going back under Angel's chin, and her bright red lipstick, which she said she had on only so she could keep track of how many times she'd kissed me and where she'd done it the most. Though she didn't actually kiss me all that often. Her whole face was just bright red lips and pale skin with those pimples lined up under her chin. No other makeup. At times I saw she had a kind of garish, too-in-love smile on her face, which I knew was only the exaggerated version of any real pleasure she was feeling. I knew that exaggeration: it was also a kind of sarcasm, meant to conceal and undercut anything she thought was too pleasurable to communicate to me without ruining it—turning it to mush—and it was meant to communicate that pleasure frankly, too. I understood. There was no other way to show that, and nothing else on her face to confuse it with.

We left town in the middle of that afternoon, with no plan except to go a few hundred miles and sleep again. Angel tried reading to me from my psychology book while I drove.

"You know, he looks like you," she said, pointing at the cover of the book. There was a picture of the statue of David next to the author's name. "Doug Douglas," she said. "What a couple of jokers his parents must have been . . ."

"That's Michelangelo's 'David'," I said, still looking at the book cover.

"I know what it is. I went to college too, you know. You aren't so much smarter."

"No smarter at all," I said. Angel had told me previously about going to Drexel University, but I always forgot. She had done well, she said. She just didn't know what she wanted to study. She went home too often, and never fit in. Junior year, when it came time to choose a major she picked history, then she was disappointed. She stopped studying, failed a midterm, and dropped out. There was a boyfriend involved. Once she'd had plans to return, but they never amounted to anything.

"He doesn't look at all like me," I said. "Look at the size of his hands."

"Not his hands," she said. "His expression."

"What about it?"

"It's just like you all the time. Like, who the hell knows what's going on in your head, but it sure looks like a good time in there. That little, cheery smile, God knows what it's supposed to mean."

"That's like me?"

She nodded and opened the book. "You, exactly," she said. "I couldn't have done it better myself." She read, "'The child's earliest, most undifferentiated sense of identity occurs at the hands of the maternal person. Here the infant receives his earliest impressions of a divine or hallowed presence manifested in the mother's breast. Later experiences in love, reverence, and admiration will evoke that initial impression and the hallowed presence of the breast as well, transformed now to the highest object of moral identification.'" She paused. "Where do they get the nerve," she said quietly. "Babies—they're talking about breastfeeding, for crying out loud."

"Right," I said. "Psychologists are more into that than you and I can imagine."

"Why is it underlined?"

I tried to get a look at the passage she had opened to, but she pulled away from me. "Probably means I needed to read it again," I said.

"No, it means it turned you on," she said.

"Whatever you say."

She flipped to another page and read something about religion and how it had lost its actual power of presence in the world. There was something about younger, bottle-fed generations not being able to invent a good enough form of reverence to reflect their shared world view.

"Blah, blah, blah. More about babies and breasts again," she said. "I really doubt that many infants are so blissful. What do they think? Babies cry all the time because they know. Life stinks."

"Well, he has a chapter on that," I said. "It's later on."

"Good for him. I'm glad. Why is this one underlined?"

"I liked it," I said.

"God," she said, and tossed the book over her shoulder into the backseat. "Enough of that. Let's sing a song."

"Sure," I said. "What songs do you know?"

"Lots of them." She paused. "Here's one. It's a round my sisters and I used to sing when we were younger. If you learn your part then we can sing it together and it's really pretty."

She cleared her throat and started singing, stopped to adjust the key because she had started too low, and went on. The words of the song were about a woman named Marjorie who needed to feed her old black sow on a cold winter morning. When she sang her voice made me think of a glass. It was just the thinnest container of something, and not the thing itself. It was a way of looking in at her, though I couldn't really be sure what I was looking at—the glass or what was inside it. There was her amusement with herself, which, I thought, was really a kind of self-confidence. I heard that, and the nervous way she had of being affectionate. She held a pitch, and by the third or fourth time around she was singing fairly loudly. I tried to sing along, and soon we were singing the parts together, circling one over the other. The tune itself was too sad to like—minor and mournful sounding, and very simple. We sang it most of that night, the rest of the way across Iowa, and later to put each other to sleep.

THAT NIGHT, in the middle of the night, I woke up and realized Angel wasn't in bed with me. The light was on in the bathroom, and without thinking, I went in there to see what she was doing. She stood in front of the mirror with nothing on, examining her breasts—one arm raised, the other hand rubbing circles around her nipple like there was something just underneath that she wanted to have.

"Angel?" I said. I looked at myself in the reflection. My eyes were comically squinted in the light, and my hair was flattened on one side from the way I had been sleeping on it. I looked back at her. "Are you all right?" I asked.

"I'm fine. I thought I felt something, but . . ." She looked at me in the mirror, still massaging herself. Then she stopped and crossed her arms, covering herself with her hands. "I can't find it," she said. "I know. Don't I know what time it is? All that talk about *breasts*—it finally gets you thinking." She leaned over the sink with her face right up to the mirror, opened her lips, and clenched her teeth, inspecting them. She had big straight teeth and her gums were pale pink. "Have you ever thought, this is just like what the rest of your skull will look like after you're dead?" she asked. She tapped her fingernail against the fronts of her teeth.

"I can't say I've had that particular thought. No."

"It might be more yellow, I think."

"It might," I said. "What are you doing?"

"Nothing. I just couldn't sleep." She looked back at me and closed her lips. "I can't stop thinking, but I didn't want to bother you, either."

"Oh well," I said.

Then she was studying my reflection with a conscious suggestion of something I hadn't expected—measuring a response she thought I was supposed to have had to her, her hips and legs as she leaned away from her reflection, turning her face from side to side in the mirror.

"Now I'm awake," I said. I rubbed my eyes and tried to smooth my hair back, grinning at her.

"You want to watch me, don't you."

"Watch you do what?" I asked.

"Finish," she said, glancing down at her reflection to remind me what she had been doing before I came into the bathroom.

"Oh. Not really." This was true. I couldn't see what she was up against with herself and her reflection, but I knew it wasn't my place to watch. It seemed more clinical than erotic. And after what she had said about her teeth being like her skull I wasn't feeling really interested in sex. "No, I don't," I said.

"Well, that's too bad."

"It isn't a show."

"It can be," she said. She stood back from her reflection

and resumed massaging, her fingers pushing up and down on her other breast, and her eyes fixed there with no expression I could read.

"I don't get this," I said. "I mean, now, in the middle of the night, you want to give yourself a breast exam." I shook my head, then went to the toilet, raised the seat and stood there, pissing.

"Did you ever find out why your mother tried to kill herself?" she asked.

I caught myself in the mirror looking as surprised by her question as I was. She hadn't stopped what she was doing, and she wasn't looking back at me. I heard piss splash on the rim of the toilet and had to look away again. "Yes, actually. I did. Why?"

"You have to tell me."

"No, not now I don't. Right now—"

"Why not?"

"—I'm going back to bed," I said, and went past her, pausing to touch her waist. I watched her in the mirror looking back at me as I did this, and saw how much she was transforming me as she looked—how she was making me up again in her mind so that I might satisfy some longing she had. I wasn't myself in this picture if I saw it the way she did; I was her watching herself, and I disliked that. Then I looked back at myself and realized how I was doing the same thing to her, in ways I didn't understand. What was between us was all our impressions of each other, with only an indistinguishable proportion of what was really there thrown in, and who could say anything about that?

"I'll tell you tomorrow," I said, and kept going.

Moments later she shook me awake again. "I can't be alone all night," she said. "Don't do this to me."

"No," I said. "What am I doing?"

"You're sleeping. You're not here."

"I'm right here."

We lay there staring at each other with nothing coming clear. All I wanted was to sleep again and let the pieces of my mind fall out of place—back to where I could believe there was nothing more required of me in the world.

"Why don't we save it, talk in the morning?" I said. "Guarantee we'll both feel better then."

"I don't feel bad," she said. "I'm jealous."

"Jealous? What of?"

"I don't know. I need you," she said. "Just be awake with me." She moved closer, yawned suddenly, and let out a breath. "I don't know. I hate it when this happens. It's so stupid. Keeping myself awake . . . being awake because I'm awake." She yawned again. "Actually, this is better. If you're patient and you don't act like you're trying to do anything, you might just put me to sleep."

"Fine."

"Then again, you could always come make love to me."

"I thought you were worried about cancer."

"I am," she said. "Death and cancer and sex." She smiled a little at the end of this, seeing the melodrama as it came into words. "So, what's wrong with feeling sorry for yourself, if no one else will? It's not like I'm having fun."

"I feel sorry, all right. I just want to sleep," I said.

"You don't know."

"I don't know. You don't know either." I touched her forehead. "Everything is out of perspective. You're tired. That's why you should forget it and go to sleep."

"I'm perfectly in perspective and I know exactly what I want. I—"

"Shh, shh, shh," I said and got up on my elbows to kiss her. Her mouth was salty and warm—softer than I had expected, her lips opening around mine. "Okay?" I asked, and kissed her again. It was like falling into something. "You're an addiction," I said. "You know that?"

She pulled me against her. I was surprised how strong her arms were, holding me there. "I've been alone all my goddamn life," she said. "Not like you. Remember that."

We were awake most of that night, too, making love in ways that confused me. Sometimes I thought there were two of her, and many more hands than mine on her body. Then I thought I had fallen asleep again and I was only dreaming the whole thing, floating through it and around it and making it up in my mind. But there were always the physical elements to check this: my sore wrists, the feeling of all her weight on my stomach or my calves, our skin sticking where it shouldn't, and the real final effort involved in breaking us apart. I remember a half-conscious tug of war over some sheets early the next morning—then curling down hard against the mattress, as far from her as possible with one leg over the cool edge of the bed, wishing I were alone, asleep, away from her and everything else in the world.

But when I woke up she was half on top of me again, asleep with one of her legs between mine, and I had no idea how we had gotten like that. She had stolen most of the covers, and had the corner of one especially pilled blanket in a fist under her chin. Her mouth was open and she was snoring. I thought the freckles on her cheeks were like the faded original pieces of her girl's face, showing her first pigmentation, where it had been and how it had broken up.

"Angel," I said. I leaned over and pulled her shoulder back and forth. Her eyebrows wrinkled together. "Wake up," I said. She sucked in a breath, swallowed once, and burrowed at her pillow. "Wake up," I said again. "Checkout is in an hour."

"I'm awake," she said. She licked her lips. "All right. Lay off my shoulder."

JOLENE'S OTHER LIFE

Jolene lived in the Richmond district, where there were views of the beach and the park, though I never saw either one from any of her windows. The whole time Angel and I were there, Richmond was fogged in, while the rest of the city was only overcast. This was fog like I had never seen. It came and wrapped around the street outside with shapes moving in it that looked solid enough to catch hold of. Jolene's apartment was a studio with a kitchen and bath, on the top floor of a large Victorian. Parts of the house were also hers to share with the other people who lived there: a downstairs living room, cellar, den, and so on. While we were there she slept in the living room and let us have the studio. I tried to talk her out of this at first but she had decided long before we arrived that this was how things would be arranged, and there was no changing it.

Jolene was thriving. She said so. When we got there she walked back out into the street with us, to be sure we had parked legally and to see the car we had come in. The door to her house was wide and heavy, with vertical panels and a brass knocker. I remember her sliding around it, closing it behind her like she wanted to hide something or keep something inside from escaping—heat, I supposed—then hugging us both and standing there on the landing, shivering. She had on a sweatshirt and jeans. I saw how nervous she was—how coming outside with us and all the things she said on the way back to the car were part of some program she had devised to make everything go just the way she wanted. She pointed out the way from the end of her street back to 101, and then told us how to get downtown. She said San Francisco was the one city she knew where you could really do something for yourself. No one got in your way here, she said, if you didn't let them. And you didn't have to go around feeling guilty that you had chosen to be so single-minded and allow yourself all the freedom in the world to follow your life's true ambitions. This was what mattered, she said. And now she could safely say she was starting to feel like a really happy person, inside and out.

"All that time you knew me, Charlie, what was I doing with myself, anyway? I hardly remember," she said.

I told her I didn't remember either, though looking at her I remembered everything. I was leaning back against Angel's car with my hands in my pockets. It was late and we'd been driving around the south side of the city for hours, lost. Angel was next to me holding her jacket closed around her and leaning toward Jolene like she wanted to be sure she didn't miss anything.

"Did you eat?" Jolene asked.

I nodded. Angel said, "In Sausalito."

"Cheap," I said, and rolled my eyes. "Big detour. That was Angel's idea. Dinner by the water."

"Just look at you," Jolene said. "Look how you turned out. Don't tell me. I know—I haven't changed a bit, right? Same youthful face?"

"Just the same," I said.

"Liar," she said, and smiled. She looked to Angel for confirmation, but Angel wasn't going to get involved.

In truth, there wasn't much difference in Jolene. Her face was still thin, and all the angles of it clear to see even in the dull light of the street lamp. There were a few more wrinkles around her eyes, and some new hardness in her upper lip that made the rest of her mouth look as if it might have slipped out of place. Her skin seemed softer than I remembered and this contributed to the slipped look as well. At the time I thought this was mostly a trick of the light, and I could easily adjust for it, making her back into what I remembered, then later it was impossible to say what my first impressions of her had been without remembering all those adjustments, exaggerating them, and picturing Jolene as a much older woman. The biggest difference, I thought, was how concerned she seemed about something I'd think of her—how she kept looking at me like she expected me, even wanted me, to think the worst of her, and I wasn't sure why that was. It was nothing like the kind of self-consciousness I remembered about her from before.

"You *look* like you're thriving," I said.

"Oh," she said. "Well, that's just me. My attitude. I try to stay positive about my life, even when I probably shouldn't. But tell me, you never said what brings you both all the way here across the country."

I thought it was appropriate that she should ask this, then, while we were all still outside in the dim light with the fog whipping around us. It put the question in another perspective, regardless of how we answered, and that made me want to laugh. Why would anyone travel thousands of miles to be cold outside on a street corner like any other street corner in the world? Anything you did could seem this arbitrary, and in that case, nothing really mattered, so why try to find any explanations? But I could see Jolene wasn't thinking along these lines. She wanted a real answer. There was something amusingly urgent and excited about the look on her face, like she had just asked one of us to dance. But we had no answer to give her—either real or rehearsed. In all the discussions of Jolene that Angel and I had ever had, the one thing we never considered was how to present ourselves to her.

"We had to find ourselves," I said, and snorted.

"Oh," Angel said. "No. We just felt like it. He talks so much about you I had to see for myself. See what I'm up against." This was probably as close to the truth as either of us could have come, but Jolene rejected it, looking sourly at me like I had tried to play a hurtful trick on her, and she would never go for it.

"Hell, you talk more about her than I do," I said to Angel.

"What?" Angel said.

"Well. I see," Jolene said. "Don't fight about it. Now you have to come in and meet everyone." And she pulled me away up the stairs with my arm held firmly under hers. Angel said something about getting some of her stuff inside, and I said that was okay. I heard the back of the car go up. Jolene leaned into me as we walked and said, "She's gorgeous, Charlie. A brunette! Why didn't you say something about you two? You might have let me in on it." She squeezed my arm under hers to keep me from moving away. I felt her breath move in my ear as she said this. "How did you do it?" she asked.

"Do what?" I said.

"She's just *right* for you. Tell the truth. You two are going to get married, aren't you."

"No," I said. "We're friends. We like each other."

"You like each other," she said. "That's nice." Then we were in a room full of people, mostly younger than Jolene, sitting in front of a television and passing around a bowl of popcorn. On the television two Hispanic children batted a blue ball back and forth between them over a net, and a man was talking, documentary style. Jolene's friends were not very impressed that I had come all this distance to see her, though Jolene seemed to imply in her introduction that they should be and soon they were smiling politely and telling me their names and professions: David and Saul who had a travel business together; Susan who was a paralegal; Anthony who didn't have a job and was looking; Henry who worked for David and Saul, typing; Jane and Alison who didn't say what they did.

"Angel," I said. "Where's Angel?"

Jolene gave me a look like I must be confused. "Outside," she said. "Getting her suitcase because you weren't polite enough to offer."

"I mean your Angel," I said. "Angelica what's-her-name—your girlfriend."

"Oh," she said, and leaned closer, "that's a long story. I'll tell you all about it." She said this quietly, then she told everyone to say who they were one more time because Angel had made it up the stairs and was standing there out of breath with a bag on her shoulder.

That night Angel and I had a discussion that came close to an argument. It began with Angel wanting to know what I thought of Jolene and seeing her. She was using a sweetened tone of voice, like she meant to comfort me, though I knew this was only so she could have leverage getting at the questions that most concerned her. "The way you put your hands on her hips, when you hugged her," she said. "That wasn't right. You know that. It wasn't like old friends. It was prurient. Did you know that?"

"I didn't," I said, and tried to remember. I thought I'd been trying to keep Jolene at a distance when I greeted her. "I mean, there's a history."

"I know there is," she said.

"Look, I could sit here and say the same things to you. She's as likely to go for you as me. I mean, I'm outclassed if it comes to that. Think of the implications—how much you've always been interested in her. The way she was looking at you, too, like . . . that's what I noticed. You heard how many times she said you were gorgeous. And I notice you don't really discourage her."

"That's disgusting, Charlie, and you know it. That's *not* me."

"Lower your voice," I said. Jolene's bed was a futon on a makeshift frame of two-by-fours, tucked in an alcove where the ceiling sloped to the floor. At our feet was a low window that rattled when the wind blew. Through the door and a short distance down the hall Jolene was visiting the two gay men who shared a studio apartment that was the mirror image of hers. I heard voices and occasional words coming from there, and bursts of affected laughter.

"I don't like this," I said. "She could hear. I just don't want to make any waves, you know."

"Personally, I think it's very entertaining. But you still haven't answered my question."

"What question."

"What you think of Jolene."

Angel was on her side facing me, with her head propped up in one hand. On the bed was a thick multicolored quilt, which Jolene had made. The outer cloth was old and stiff and smelled clean. Jolene had explained about it—what the quilt meant and where the different scraps had come from, why she chose them, but I hadn't been paying much attention at that point.

"Honestly, I think she's troubled," I said. "Always was, always will be. But I like her."

"I'll bet you do. And you'd probably screw her again in a second, too."

I winced and glanced away at the ceiling right next to my head. I put my hand there. The paneling was warmer than I had expected. I pictured Jolene in this bed, which was not the bed she and I had ever shared, and tried to think of a way to answer Angel, who seemed on the verge of a jealous fit. She was doing a good job of concealing it—but ostentatiously so. She wanted me to know how upset she was and to feel responsible for it. But that only limited the ways I had of answering her, which was obviously not what she wanted. She wanted the truth. "I could do that," I said. "Yes, I am attracted to her, and I could imagine doing that. Of course I can. I just don't think she's interested, and neither am I. You can control these things when they aren't the smartest thing to do. I mean, it's over with Jolene and me."

"Bull," she said, and we went back and forth on that point for a while—why was I attracted and how much was I attracted, what attracted meant, and so on.

"I'll leave you two alone tomorrow," she said. "That's it. Then you can have it out, and see what you like about her so much."

"But I'm not interested," I said.

"'But I'm not interested,'" she said. "Tell me about it."

"What about her girlfriend?" I asked.

"No sign of her interfering, either."

I lay back next to her and tried to imagine a way of letting the whole thing go. I sighed and stared straight up. "Well, we didn't get the picture very well, though, did we," I said. "I mean, Jolene's other life."

"Shut up. I'm not talking to you about it."

"No millionaire art dealers," I said.

"No," she said. "No Planned Parenthood, either."

"Wrong part of town, too."

"What part of town?"

"Where we thought she would live. In the Haight."

"Oh. Right. I think that exhibit sounds really stupid," she said. "What kind of people is it supposed to appeal to?"

"Berkeley people," I said, and rolled toward her. "All those hip, enlightened Berkeley types who like to go to the Oakland Musem and see themselves reflected in hip, artistic ways."

"Shut up," she said. "What do you know about any of that?"

"I'm just guessing."

"'Women in Their Own Image,'" she said. I could tell she was more interested in this than she would let on. "I forget. Is that what it's called?"

"That was it, I think."

"No, it isn't. It had to with the media," she said.

"Right."

"For women," she said, scornfully. "For women by women. Give me a break. How come I'm a woman and I feel excluded? What is that supposed to mean?"

"I don't know. Maybe if you saw it you would like it. Maybe you'd see yourself and suddenly be validated, like that." I snapped my fingers.

"Oh shut up," she said. Then we were both laughing quietly. "No," she said, "I'll tell you what it is, it's that common form of reverence—having a coherent faith, like what I was reading to you in that book the other day. Like, 'I don't have anything to believe in so I think I'll believe in myself.'"

I laughed. "People are paying big money, though," I said. "That foundation she works for is big money."

"What do you care about it?"

"I don't."

All the heat in the house seemed to go to the one corner where Angel and I lay. Soon we were on top of the covers, sweating and chilly at the same time because of the draft blowing through the window. Angel was still on her side, facing me, and I could almost see through the nightgown she had on. I couldn't remember what her ankles were like, whether they were thin in the ways I remembered, and where the veins went through them. I was trying to remember this when she asked me what I was thinking about.

"About your ankles," I said.

"Hah," she said. "Mine or someone else's?"

"Yours," I said, and stared hard at her. "You."

"Why?"

"Because you're so beautiful."

I expected she would want to put this off and argue with me, like she did most of the time when I tried to compliment her. But she didn't.

"Really?" she said.

"Like now," I said. "I look at you, and I just don't even know where to start."

"What do you mean—start?"

"Where to start to touch you."

"Where do you want?" Her voice was high and thin sounding, like it often got when we approached this point of intimacy—assertive, with a little fear going under that. I thought, if she was afraid at all it wasn't because of anything I might do to hurt her; it was all the the unmentioned ways she was afraid I would overlook her—everything about her I might not notice, and that she didn't want to have to point out to me.

"Well," I said, and put my hand low on her stomach. I felt her breath go in and out. "It's just like I said. I don't know. I don't know where."

"What if I let you just this once do anything you could think of."

"What?"

"If I let you? Show me what you do."

I waited, thinking about it. "I'm at a loss," I said. "You can't let me do anything. What I feel—that's all in *my* head."

"Come on, Charlie," she said softly. "Just have me however you want. What do you want?" She closed her eyes and feigned an expression like she was about to pass out. "Don't you want me?" she asked, and smiled.

"Yes," I said. "Very much." I put my hands around her neck and squeezed lightly.

"Don't," she said. "No more talking." She got up and lifted her nightgown over her head, then stood over me and beside the bed with her arms up against the slope of the ceiling and her legs apart. Strands of light came through the blinds in the window and went up her leg, blending and changing shape on her hips as she moved, always just outside my touch every time I reached for her. I saw, or saw what I could imagine just beyond my reach, glistening between her legs. I lunged halfway out of the bed at her and pulled her down.

"Ouch." She was slapping the sides of my head. "That tickles."

"And you'd think we'd be sick of this by now," I said. "Every day."

"Not *every* day," she said. "Almost." Then she was sinking onto me, dramatically limp, letting me have her. "Take me, take me, Romeo, oh take me," she said. I ended up on my knees on the floor, between her legs, while she lay back on the bed. She was wary at first and said she couldn't see any good reason for me to want to do this. "It's gross," she said, but eventually she wasn't talking at all. She would sit up over me and squeeze the sides of my head, then lie down again, breathing hard and whispering things I couldn't understand. I was certain that all my pleasure had to come through her; this way her pleasure would be partially mine, and I would know what that was like. In the end it was almost what I had wanted. I felt it with my hands, how her orgasm began in the center of her chest, in some tension where her ribs joined—a muscular tightening that spread to the root of her stomach, where I felt it double. I was pushing down with my hands as firmly as she pushed back to feel how it grew and came loose from her, turning to paroxysms in her hips and flashes of heat and shudders that wracked her whole body and seemed like they would not end. When I came on top of her she never said anything. She was still and wet with sweat, a fluid motion against me, open to me. I had my whole weight on her, my hands through hers, and our arms were out as far as we could reach.

"That was very different. You may not believe it, but no one's ever done that to me," she said when it was over. Then she seemed to think I had misunderstood her. "I mean I liked it. A lot." I was surprised at how quickly she turned back into herself, using real words again to describe what had happened, though I knew this should not be surprising; it made no sense, but I felt almost betrayed by her lucidity. "I think we should just keep making it a little different, like that, every time. That could be a lot of fun. But I don't want to get so completely centered on me."

"Sure," I said.

Then she was asleep, but it was a while before I slept. I was awake there on Jolene's pillow imagining the things I couldn't smell or hear all through her house and going back over the faces of the people she lived with to see if there was anything I had missed about them, but I didn't remember well enough. I wanted to have a reason to be there, lying in her bed with Angel, but I had none. I didn't feel like an intruder either. I thought I was entitled. In fact, I felt like I had come here mostly because of that. I just couldn't quite see what I was entitled to. I wanted

Jolene to know what I'd become and how I'd grown up—
that was part of it. But there was more. I wanted to break
her. If I tried to picture Jolene exactly the way I wanted to
leave her when we left, this is what I saw: her sitting up
on this bed, alone for days, crying. Ruined. I knew the
picture was probably as cruel as it was unrealistic, and I
tried to talk myself out of it, but there it was.

When I woke up late the next morning Angel wasn't in
bed, and there was a note sitting on top of my pants
where I'd let them fall on the floor the night before. It
said, "See you tonight, sometime. A—," with "sometime"
underlined. It was only a few minutes after I'd read this
and retreated under the covers to sleep a little more when
Jolene came in.

"Sorry to barge in," she said. She had on the same plaid
bathrobe she'd always worn. "I'll be just a sec." She stood
across the room from me in the light from the window
over her bureau with her back turned, picking things out
of the drawers. She stood on one foot, the other foot
moving impatiently up and down against her bare calf,
the cartilage clicking. "That's the nice thing about this job
where I am now—I can show up whenever I want. Put in
my thirty hours. No one cares when. So, here I am, nine-
thirty, bright and not so early," she said. "Nice, isn't it?"
She slid the bureau drawer shut and turned around to
face me.

"Yes," I said.

I saw, again, how her face hadn't really changed. Some part of what went under the surface of her expressions was more visible, maybe—unfairly exposed, like time had left certain secrets stranded in her face so long she couldn't remember how to hide them. Then again, it might as easily be an effect I was having on her. She was shocked to see me. She wasn't used to me the way I now was. And I knew she was well aware I hadn't missed this, either, which made her even more uncomfortable. "Where's your girlfriend?" she asked, and touched her wrist to her forehead nervously, then dropped it back to hold the clothes she had draped over her arm.

"Danged if I know," I said, and leaned out of the bed to snatch her note up off the floor. I tossed this at Jolene. It caught in the air and fell short. "Guess she had something to do today."

"Something to do?" she asked.

I shrugged.

"So, does this mean I'll be seeing more of you?"

"As much as you like," I said.

She came and sat at the end of the bed then, stopping to pick up Angel's note, which she glanced over and placed on my leg. Then she leaned forward to brush something away from her toes and sat back, straining to see across the room. "You could come to the museum for part of the day," she said. "I don't have anything really important until later on, when I have a meeting with some people. I can tell you the interesting places to visit in Oakland."

"Sure," I said. "Sounds fun."

"I mean, it isn't the greatest town in the world," she said, and smiled. "Not like here. Kind of a drive, too. That's only temporary, though, thank God—till we get the exhibit set. Then I'm back in the offices over here." She pointed one of her long fingernails at her leg, like she meant the offices were on her knee.

"Huh," I said. I was determined not to let her talk to me about unmeaningful things like offices or sights to see in the city. "That sounds fine."

"Good," she said.

"My mother said you told her you were going to get your tubes tied," I said. She stiffened a little but never let go of her smile. She looked like one of those pictures of herself in my mother's desk—a little nervous and charmed. "Why is that?" I asked. "Technically you don't really have to."

"Technically I most certainly do," she said. "I'm as liable to bear children now as ever before." She looked like she wanted me to see she was sorry for me in a way I would never understand, and endeared at the same time. "No. The thing is, I have no intentions now or ever of being somebody's *mother*." She smiled as she said that word, as if it were something obviously ridiculous. "I'm just trying to live with the idea," she said. "To see what

I want. I don't expect anyone to understand, least of all Mary."

"Then why don't you tell her that?" I asked. "Write her. She thinks you're mad at her."

"I will." She scratched her head and continued. "You're right, I owe her a letter. Just between you and me, I think she's afraid I have designs on her. That's why I haven't written. It's a little insulting."

"You don't," I said.

"Of course not. What a crazy idea. You trust a friend enough to tell her about this decision you've made about your life, your sexuality, and she treats it like you're a rabid dog or something. My God, stay away, stop the spread of contamination, don't come near me. It's ridiculous. Like the last thing in the world I would be attracted to is some neurotic woman who can't stand the sight of her own shadow. Think about it, realistically. I mean, don't get me wrong, Charlie; I love your mother dearly. Just not like that."

"I see," I said. I thought this defense was too overstated not to be connected with other things she wasn't going to tell me. I had forgotten how good Jolene was at using a little drama to avoid whatever she didn't quite know how to tell you. "I wonder how much you're reading into that, though."

"Nothing at all. Believe me, there have been some pretty heated exchanges—pretty hard to misinterpret."

"Wow," I said. "She never mentioned it."

"She wouldn't." Jolene said.

"Huh. So. Then, tell me all about Angelica."

"You know, that still isn't easy," she said, and that was all.

"Why, what happened?"

"Not a whole lot, as it turns out." She leaned forward, like she was about to get up. "You don't want to know."

"Why not?"

"You don't." She stood up then, pulled all her hair over one shoulder, and looked down at me, smiling. "It's just so good to see you." I smelled all the usual smells that clung to her—a little deeper and stronger than I remembered them, which I imagined had something to do with her being older now. For a moment her bathrobe was open halfway up her leg. "It's too bad about Angel—your Angel," she said, sounding genuinely sorry, though that most likely had to do with something else: more drama. I couldn't see what there was for her to be so sorry about. "I'd like to know her a little better."

"You will. She's just being generous," I said. "Her idea of generous. She said something about it last night, and I didn't actually believe her. She thought we'd want to catch up or something."

"Oh, nice," she said. "I'll just go get dressed over at David's." She pointed with her chin. "Then we can eat here and go." She left the room.

I lay there awhile, unable to stay awake because of the

heat, and letting myself spin in and out of consciousness while I looked around Jolene's room and tried to imagine her in it. There was a yellow hardwood floor that was polished and gleaming; a cream colored throw rug with blue fringe at the center of the room beside the couch; her old desk and stereo and TV all in a line on one wall; and her bureau, which was wide and tall with curly handles in front and decorative wings along the top. That was at the wall farthest from me, with a window over it. I imagined Jolene sitting at that desk—how she would be hunched slightly to one side, then she would lean back and stretch. I thought of a few things like that—Jolene walking back and forth across her apartment, reading on the couch, and so on—then I forced myself awake and went into the bathroom for a shower.

The tiles there were all white and dull from soap, and there were twelve different shampoos to choose from in the glass stall shower. While I waited for the water to heat up, smelling the soap and steam and watching myself vanish in the mirror over the sink, I noticed a framed picture hanging above the toilet. It was a small painting of a shadowy naked woman with long legs seen from behind, leaning against a bureau like Jolene's. It wasn't a very good painting. The brush strokes were unsure, too globbed and not at all even. But there was a kind of intensity about it that I liked, and I figured this was what Jolene had picked it for. The window in front of the woman was open, with a breeze moving the curtains. The longer I looked, the more I liked it. Then I realized the painting was actually done in Jolene's room. I thought it must be Jolene in the picture—something some lover of hers had done for her. On a closer look, though, I saw it wasn't Jolene at all, but someone with darker hair shaped much like her. I was right next to the picture then, with one knee up on the toilet seat, to see better. She was looking back over her shoulder, straight at me, as if she were tired, or about to suggest something. There was pencil writing underneath that looked fairly fresh. It said "In the Morning," and under that were Jolene's initials, JAS. I had no trouble making that out. And though there was no way in the world for me to say who it was Jolene had painted in that picture, I realized suddenly why she looked so familiar: she was altogether too much like my mother.

JOLENE DESCRIBED the exhibit for me on our way to Oakland that morning. She said it attempted to deal with an idea that certain powerful men in our society had been selling to people for years: that all women are essentially narcissistic, in love with themselves for a lot of false images men have generated, and entirely reliant on those images to know anything about themselves. She said a few things about power. Then she said, "The way it works out, women don't have their own idea of themselves anymore. There's the collective self-image of that

other woman—the unattainable one on the billboards or
the Diet Coke ads that *men* like so much. But that's not
us. We want the image back. We want that picture in the
water back, clear—the way it really is." She straightened
one hand, palm down, on the steering wheel like she was
flattening something under it. "Don't get me wrong. I
know things aren't much easier, being a man these days.
God knows, but, then again, who's been running the show
for years?"

"Not me," I said.

"I know, not you." She smiled and shook her head. "Of
course, not you. It's so easy to seem like you're over-
stating yourself when you try to talk about this. You
understand."

"Sure I do," I said. "I'm with you all the way." As long as
she paid this much attention to the way men felt about
her she was going to be stuck with them, even if only by
opposition. But I wasn't going to get into that with her—
why it was so, or what it meant. "That's the theme," I said.
"So what are some of the pieces like? Tell me."

"All self-portraits," she said. "Various media. We've
asked artists from across the country to give us their
strongest self-portraits—something like what they think
sums up all the ways they see themselves. In the end, you
get a picture—a whole collaborative self-image. What
women really see. How these women, anyway—who are
smart and in a way successful at seeing, after all—see

themselves, not in someone else's image, but their own."
She glanced across the seat at me. We were stopped at a
light then. "But you didn't come all this way to have a lecture on art. I know that."

"No," I said, and the light changed.

"Tell me about yourself," she said, and gazed straight
ahead. She had warned me that we wouldn't be getting
any of the views of San Francisco or seeing any of the
nicer parts of town on our way to Oakland. To our right
were rundown Victorians, and newer, square apartment
buildings going up steep streets to hilltops that didn't
seem level enough to be built on. On the left was a green
park with ragged-looking trees—palms, eucalyptus, and
shrubby pines.

"Nothing to tell."

"Maybe we could go through Chinatown, over Broadway," she said, and then made a face like she disagreed
with herself about this.

"That'd be fine."

"No," she said. "Too far. Tell me something. What do
you do now?"

"Retail. I sell shirts. Actually, when we get back I'm going
to try something else, I think. I don't know. Maybe school."

"Ah-ha. You quit, or you lost your job?"

I nodded, smiling. "A little of both. We just kind of
left. So, technically we quit, yes, but then again they'd be
happy to fire us for what we did if we tried to go back."

"And this is where Angel works too?"

I nodded. "Worked."

We didn't say anything else for a while. The street leveled off at each intersection as we went downhill. Soon we were in another neighborhood where there were many darker, more attractive stone apartment buildings with shops and cafés on the bottom floors. It began to rain, not heavily—big drops that splashed on the windshield.

"Jolene," I said. It was the first time I had said her name out loud to her, and I liked the effect. I wanted to say it again. "Jolene. There are so many things to talk about."

"There sure are."

"What did you do when you left Connecticut?"

"I came right out here," she said. "I struggled awhile. Temping, word-processing, stuff like that." She made a face. "I even tried out at this one place to deliver singing telegrams—can you believe it? I can't *sing*." She looked at me and laughed as if this were startling.

"Really."

"Then I found the house, and I started to work for the foundation, representing them in different museums. That was 1978, spring. It's been about the same ever since."

"Is that how you met Angelica—at work?"

She didn't answer right away. The rain was getting heavier now. "You already asked about her," she said. She rolled down her window and adjusted the sideview mirror, then turned on her windshield wipers and glanced nervously across the seat at me and out the window. She put her hand up to my face, half-curled and barely touching me, and said, "I see a face inside a face when I look at you. I like that—the way you are now. It's just right, I guess; you turned out just right. But I still see that other face in there and I don't know what to think of it."

"Whose face?"

"Yours. When I used to know you."

Then she was distracted, making a left turn at a busy intersection with the light going yellow. Someone rushed at us from the opposite side of the intersection, sounding his horn. Jolene glanced hatefully after him and swung into traffic.

"Whose picture is that hanging in the bathroom?" I asked. She didn't answer. "You painted it, right? But I can't tell who it is."

The windshield wipers squeaked back and forth. The rain was letting up. "Why are you grilling me about this?" she asked.

"I'm not."

"It's not any of your business."

"Funny thing," I said. "That's just exactly what she said before I left. She said, Don't meddle."

"Now you're really confusing me."

"I am?"

"Yes! Who said not to meddle?"

"The woman in the picture—"

"Oh, really?"

"—my mother. Did you even forget we were related?"

Without signaling or looking at me she pulled the car up sharply on the curb in front of a Mexican restaurant with a long yellow sign in front that said Barzabo's. It was dark in the front window, not open yet; there was a motel called Happy End next to that with a narrow driveway and shrubbery in front, and a young balding man wearing a cheap shirt sitting inside at a desk and twirling a pencil around in his fingers. Another man went by in a ripped coat, pushing a shopping cart and spitting invisible things on the sidewalk as he walked. At first I thought he was cursing because we'd almost run him over, but I saw, as he kept walking, that his rage really had nothing to do with us, or anything you might be able to see.

Jolene left the car running. "What in the world are you talking about?" she said.

"I'm talking about you and my mother."

She looked straight down into her lap. She took her hands off the steering wheel and rubbed one up and down on her slacks a moment for no apparent reason. "Did she . . . ," she began. Then, "Crazy. This is absolutely crazy."

"It is?" I asked. "Why?"

"Look, I don't know what she's told you, but if you want the truth," she said. She looked up at me and I saw her eyes were wet now, full, like water going over the edge of a glass, and red, though she wasn't crying. She looked enraged and terrified at the same time. Then her eyes were darting all over the inside of the car and not seeming to see anything. "Charlie," she said. "How can I say this . . . there was a time when your mother and I were very close. It was never anything like that, I guess, but it had all the"—she paused—"the potential. The attraction. I thought so, anyway." She looked as if she were trying to find an answer to a question other than the one she thought I'd asked—the one I'd ask next, maybe. "I guess you could say we were close to it at times. I just didn't trust myself to know that was what it was all about. I didn't actually know." Then it looked as if the question might have turned to an accusation in her mind. "I have no idea what she's told you, but I'm sure it's a whole different story than what you'll hear from me."

I tasted cornflakes in my mouth, and the coffee I'd had for breakfast. "This was going on like this back in Farmington?" I asked, and I was surprised at the steady, low sound of my voice, almost a growl, like I was on a tape recorder going too slowly.

"Oh, yes," she said. "Nothing ever happened that you could point to and say, there it is. You know: sex. We talked about it. We talked and talked and talked and then we just never came out and said anything. Or did anything. That's my impression of it anyway. So maybe I have a sick mind. Is that what you want to hear?"

"Wait. This was before you and me. Not after."

"Oh, after that I had very little to do with your mother, and you know that. It was all so vague in my mind what it had been about, anyway. I thought that was it for that kind of a relationship. That was the extent of it, and I was a little disappointed."

"I don't understand. You were or you weren't," I paused, trying to come out with the right word. "Lovers."

"We were like that at times. Once, maybe—twice. I don't remember. I don't know if you could really say. You can't put it in these terms, Charlie, because *we* never did. They're your terms. To us it just wasn't like that."

"I don't see how that can be," I said.

"Well, try. You want to know. Last spring I met a woman, Angelica, and then I had to go through it all over again: what is this *thing* I have about certain women, being attracted. This was in a drawing class—I was trying to do a little drawing, and she was the model. And I swear, it was just lascivious, the way she looked at me. At first I was completely put off by that—I mean, who in their right mind? Who is this woman? She would look at me and, to me, it was just perverse what her eyes were doing. For a while I thought there must be something wrong with her that would make her do that. Then I thought maybe it was something wrong with me, that I was seeing it the way I was. But I don't think she actually knew. She was unaware. I mean, it wasn't actually perverse, I started to think, it was much more . . ." She did something with her hands like she was folding a cloth, "more ambiguous. It didn't have to mean anything at all—in the ways I was used to things having a meaning—though certainly it could mean that if I wanted it to. Do you see what I'm saying? And actually, she was the one to be shy about the whole thing in the end. Not me." She looked at me and seemed happy to report this, almost like she was bragging.

"You weren't," I said.

"It's embarrassing to talk about it like this with you," she said, and looked away, still smiling. "I didn't actually know I had these feelings. I mean, there was Mary, but that never went deep, and I had no idea. It was just the way this woman would look at me. Part of it was remembering how Mary and I were, once upon a time—how that never really worked. Yes." She nodded her head. "I can see now why you would make that mistake, actually, with the painting. They were sort of look-alikes. Which probably has something to do with why I wrote Mary to tell her, too. We'd been out of touch for years. But I lied. I told her Angelica was my lover already, that's all, to show her it *could* be done like I wanted, and to make her jealous because I thought that was the right thing."

"She wasn't your lover."

"Yes," she said. "She certainly was, but not for long."

"Tell me something," I said. "Does my mother know about us?"

"No," Jolene said. "Not from me she doesn't."

"Well," I said, because I had nothing else to say. I tasted more cornflakes, and suddenly I knew this meant I was going to be sick, which made no sense at all because I hadn't felt it coming until then. I didn't think I was in the kind of emotional condition that would bring it on. I was just shocked and outside of things. I had an impression of myself as someone who was getting physically narrower and narrower—that there was only so much room in me for hearing these things. "Just a minute, I'm going to throw up," I said, and I remember saying it very clearly.

I opened the door and leaned out over the sidewalk. This was familiarly disgraceful, all the pain and humiliation, like the worst days of childhood. I was hanging out of a car in a town I didn't know, puking for no apparent reason, cornflakes and coffee going up my nose and splattering on the wet ground. I thought, None of this had anything to do with me. None of it had to do with anything I could have predicted. Then it was over and I was a mess, with snot dripping off my chin.

"Give me something," I said. "Kleenex, something." And I stuck my hand out behind me without sitting up or turning around to face her. "Come on."

I heard her moving around on the seat next to me. "I

don't have anything," she said. I heard her open the glove compartment, then snap it shut. "No, I don't have anything." Then she was laughing.

"Find something," I said.

"All right." I heard her shifting around in the seat. Then a moment later there was something light and warm in my hand—one of her socks. It was damp and trampled thin on the sole. I scrubbed this across my chin and face, blew my nose in it, rolled up a corner and shoved it in my nostrils, then let it fall on the ground there and closed the car door. I sat back in the seat with my eyes shut, not moving at all. I had expected I would be dizzy when I opened my eyes, but I wasn't. I didn't even feel like I had to be sick again.

"You okay?" she asked.

"Fine. Take me back to your place. Just forget this all ever happened."

"Okay," she said. The man in the Happy End Motel was sitting up a little straighter at his desk and peering anxiously at our car like he was about to get up and ask if everything was okay, or if we needed a room after all, though it was hard to say he was actually looking at us. Jolene pulled out into the street. I crossed one leg under me on the seat and sat with my back against the door and both hands lightly on my stomach. For a moment I pictured us on a freeway somewhere, headed south, maybe, just the two of us, hot and half undressed for the sun.

Jolene would be like a gypsy, wearing a band around her forehead. Picturing this I remembered how she and I had never been able to put away all our attraction as long as we were in sight of each other—how that constant awareness of sex was the hardest part of being with her. It reduced every feeling to desire and need.

"So, which one of us did you like better," I asked. "Me or my mother?"

"I only had you, really. The way I wanted." She looked unburdened now, like some part of her had just been untied. The rain had stopped and the wind was coming through her window. She was flushed and smiling, though I couldn't see why. There was nothing pleasant on the horizon to distract her. Still, I trusted this expression as showing something close to the way she really felt. I trusted she would say whatever was closest to the truth for her—what she really meant as the truth. "It's so different, you can't really understand," she said.

"Try me."

"In the one case you're alone with someone just like you, a woman; in the other case you're alone with someone who's totally unlike you. Either way, you do the same things. Basically. It amounts to the same thing. And you're alone when it's over."

This could be only partly true, but I didn't think I needed to know about it any more than that. "And you were never lovers after us," I said. I had to ask again, since

I could now be more certain I was getting real answers from her.

"No," she said. "I said no. We barely saw each other. You know that."

"Yes, I know. You and I were close then."

"We were. And that can never change."

"Oh, yes," I said. "It has certainly changed."

ANGELICA WAS nothing like my mother. Jolene showed me pictures when we got back to her place and she realized she had to come inside with me for a new pair of socks. I think she wanted me to see those pictures so she would feel better understood—so I would have some clear or unhateful idea of what she'd become. Angelica was a big woman, with long dark hair and gray eyes. She looked heavy without being fat—just solid and very female. I imagined how cool all that skin would be to touch. The fact that in Jolene's mind this woman was anything like my mother only proved how important my mother must have been for her. She probably could have made anyone out to remind her of my mother. I didn't mention that to Jolene, though. I just said something about how she and Angelica must have been in love—this was how it looked in the pictures. There was one I remember, a little out of focus, where Angelica was thumbing her nose at Jolene and smiling. In the other ones she was much less expressive, lounging around Jolene's apartment half-dressed and looking unconcerned. In some of them it looked like she might resent having all this attention from Jolene, but I couldn't be sure.

Jolene treated us to dinner at a sushi bar that night. This was supposed to be our big send-off. We thought we would be leaving late the next day. I was silent most of that evening, distracted by the sushi man and his antics with a big, deadly looking knife, listening to the piped-in ocean sounds of some new kind of Oriental music, while Angel and Jolene talked. I tuned in and out of their conversation, which had to do with California, the differences between people here and back home. Angel had spent the day walking around San Francisco and she was convinced there were big differences, she just couldn't say for sure what they were. She had on the best clothes she'd brought, a gray jacket and matching pants from Seal and Cahn. She seemed excited in a new way—like all the differences she'd noticed in Californians had somehow come off on her, just by her noticing them. It was the first time I noticed what expressive eyebrows she had—how long and thick they were and how she moved them around to convey her wonder.

"Charlie, did you forget?" she asked. This was toward the end of our meal, which turned out not to be a meal at all but a succession of small bamboo plates with colorful rice and seaweed fish things on them, and accompanying piles of pink shredded ginger. She leaned her head down next to me and I smelled some new sharp scent like the taste of that ginger in her hair. "The present," she whispered.

"What are you talking about?" I said.

"Jolene's present."

"What are you two whispering about?" Jolene said.

"We're not," I said.

"Charlie has something for you," Angel said, and then she led my hands down under her seat, into her bag, where there was a box with a bow on it. "A Christmas present for you," she said. "Didn't he ever tell you how we met?"

"No. You met at work," Jolene said. "Right?"

"Right, when Charlie came around looking for a present for you in the women's department."

"Here," I said, and placed the box on the bar between us, in front of Angel. It was wrapped in gold foil.

"Well," Jolene said. "Then I'm not sure who should be thanking who, but I'll thank you both. Should I open it?" she asked, taking the box and shaking it with her head cocked and a silly, pleased look on her face.

"Yes," I said, and I looked at Angel for a sign—what kind of plan she had, if she had one, and whether I had done the right thing giving this box to Jolene. She just grinned at me with her eyebrows finally coming level.

Jolene unwrapped the gift. "They're beautiful," she said, pushing the box and wrappings away from her. She held up an angora bomber hat with ear flaps, much like the one I'd gotten her at the store, and a pair of small, matching gloves. "Beautiful," she said. "What a thoughtful present." She put the hat on a moment, then took it off and stroked it. "Rabbit," she said. The hat looked ridiculous and childish on her, standing up on her head like a flattened dunce cap with earflaps.

"I get a kiss," Jolene said, and before I could think she had kissed Angel twice on the mouth.

"Well," I said, and for a moment we were both leaning across Angel. Jolene caught her fingers around mine and pulled me to her. I felt something wet blow across my face and when I sat back I saw she was crying. She hid her face in the hat a moment. Then she took a deep breath and faced us again, smiling coolly but still sniffing.

"It's just so nice," she said. "I'm extremely touched. You came all this way. And I want you to know that I wish you all the best in the world. I want you both to know." She said a few other things, then, about how good we were for each other, and how glad she was to be a part of the way we had met. I thought what she said was mostly sincere, though it didn't matter at all. She was only returning a favor by rote, and the things she was wishing us were neither asked for, or hers to give. The more she said, the harder it was for me to listen.

"We'll have what we want," Angel said, finally. "Whatever we want. Together or not together, and no thanks to you." It wasn't biting or vengeful the way she said it. This was just her way of saying the one thing she had always wanted to be able to say to Jolene. "No thanks, whatsoever," she said quietly. "You have nothing to do with anything." And for a moment I was locked back into Jolene's yellow-green eyes, remembering something she had said to me once about how I was diaphanous—only the word I thought of now was "devilish," not "diaphanous," and I wasn't sure why that was.

LATER THAT night, sitting on Jolene's couch, Angel told me she had decided she would not be going home the next day. She said she didn't know when, if ever, she wanted to go back east. I was so surprised I forgot to react to this. Mostly I was too stunned to feel anything. And from the way she said it I knew she was completely serious. I said, "What will you do?" She said she would get someone—her sister, probably—to sell all her furniture, ship out her clothes, and close her bank account.

"And where will you stay?" I asked. She lay curled on her side with her feet in my lap.

"I checked that out today, too. I was pretty busy."

"Busy," I said. At least it was a familiar word—one where I could hang my usual impressions of Angel. She was busy. And I had heard over dinner some of the places she had gone. "What did you find? You found a place?" I asked.

"No, not yet. But it won't be hard. There's a share-rental bureau that gets things in every day. They set you up."

"Well. And you'll get a job, just like that," I asked, without meaning to sound as if I doubted her.

"Of course," she said. "I have money. We barely touched my money. I spoke to Debra, anyway, and she said she'll try to help out—like I said. Sell my stuff, close the account."

"I'm just finding this really hard to believe," I said. It was the expected thing to say, and I had some trouble sounding like it meant anything to me.

"Of course. That's because you haven't asked the most important question."

"What's that?" I asked.

"About you. You and me. That's what you want to know."

"But there's no point asking that," I said. "I know."

"No you don't." She laughed. "Here you are, going on about me and my money and you forget to ask the main thing—what'll happen to you."

"I'll do whatever I want," I said.

"Well, well," she said. "I was going to ask if you would stay, too. But now I'm not so sure." She laughed again, so I knew the offer was still good. Then she sat up and put her arms around my shoulders and I couldn't think at all about what was happening, or what she was saying, describing the new life she pictured for us here in San Francisco.

I pushed her away. "We spent all my money," I said.

"We'll split what's left of mine. Don't worry."

"I don't even know what it costs to fly home." I looked hard at her and couldn't see why she was acting so joyously—how real any of this was. "It just isn't what I expected," I said. "Not at all."

"We'll get you home, all right," she said. "I wish you could think about it. You know, if I end up hurting you too much—if we end up hurting each other, then I'll never be able to stand the sight of you. Not that I won't wish I could. Think of what that'll be like." She paused, waiting for me to say something. "Just think. Isn't this always the way it ends."

THAT NIGHT I dreamed about the way Jolene had kissed Angel at dinner. In my dream it went on much longer and the scenery behind them shifted several times so I could never be sure where they were. Their mouths were munching gently together, lips around lips, and I was surprised at how beautiful this was to see—the casual, almost joking way it began, and all the softness it amounted to. Their chins were flat against each other and their eyes were open—both with a kind of merry expression in them, like they were only talking. The dream was so clear it woke me up, and I lay there for a long time trying to figure out what it was about. Some kind of bliss. Angel went on sleeping.

At first I thought I was only beginning to confuse the two women, and this proved what a good thing it was Angel and I probably would not be together much longer. I didn't want them mixed up, or running together in my mind so they were like the same person. But the dream itself was too warm and undisturbing for me not to think it might mean just the opposite. It might indicate how much I was in agreement with the whole situation—how I should stay here, because everything was actually all right and out in the open. It was a kind of harmony, being with Angel and having this dream. I was awake a long time trying to see what was what, but I decided nothing.

The next day Angel and I walked all over San Francisco and talked more about what we should do. She was every bit as set on staying as I had thought she was the night before, and I was pretty sure it was the right thing for her. We went to the usual tourist attractions—the Japanese Tea Garden, Nob Hill, and Fisherman's Wharf. I remember walking somewhere along the water in the marina, past all the bright yachts there and the park that was full of people on their lunch, jogging and throwing frisbees, even though it was still cold and overcast, raining off and on. Angel was telling me about her sisters again, the one spring that Marcie had gone to a boarding school because of trouble she was having with friends at home. Angel said this was the moment she had waited for all her life—to finally grow up and take Marcie's place, do everything she did. Most of all, she said, she had wanted to be like Debra's twin. She was thirteen then, Debra was fifteen.

She said, "It never worked that way. At first I thought it was because Debra really hated me and I just wasn't living up to Marcie. There was this special thing between them and I would never have it because I wasn't good enough. But it wasn't that at all. They were like half-people, that's what I decided. They wanted whatever they could get away from each other, to be whole.

"I remember this one day, Debra and I were playing Ping-Pong and I had actually managed to score something like ten points on her. Big deal. I thought it was funny and I was laughing about it. Then I realized, Debra was really, really upset. She was so upset she wasn't even herself, she was like this . . . jerk. I don't know how to describe it. She was going to do anything she could to beat me. Then I realized that what I always thought was so great and wonderful about them was really just this insane way they were always competing, trying to get something away from each other—outdo each other because they felt incomplete having each other around. That's all. I was never jealous after that. I was glad, just to be all one whole person, you know, by myself, and I was never jealous of them again."

"Huh," I said. "Never?"

"Of course I was at times, but not in that deluded way."

We were at the end of the land. Across the bay was the Golden Gate Bridge. Where we were standing I couldn't see either foot of the bridge—one was behind a hill, the other hidden in fog—so it looked suspended in air, the whole middle section just a flying red arch of roadway coming out of the fog with nothing to hold it up.

"It's too nice out here for me anyway," I said. "I could never live in a place this nice. It's unreal." The headlands were bald and green across the water, with the fog slipping down. Sausalito glittered next to them like a town in a fantasy. Then the fog shredded slightly so I could see one missing leg of the bridge going into the water.

"I wasn't telling you that so you'd think I'm telling you to leave. You and I are nothing like that—like twins. Maybe you and Jolene . . . look." She stopped. "That just isn't what I was hoping you would say."

"What were you hoping?" I asked. I faced her and saw how uncertain this talk left her. She didn't believe I could have understood most of what she said, maybe because she didn't believe it herself, or think of it as clearly as she had described it for me. The spray and fog made sleeves of moisture that wouldn't stay around all the loose hairs framing her face, with bead-sized drips weighing these down and blowing off at places. The hair on her face was white and wet like a mask.

"That you would stay. That you'd say . . . how much do you love me, anyway?"

"How can I tell you how much?" I said, not taking my eyes away from hers.

"You can if you want. You can say you love me more than any other person in the world ever has. You can say you love me more than you've ever loved anybody else. That's the way I feel about you, you know."

"No it isn't."

"It certainly is."

I shrugged. "I'm not the only person in the world who could love you."

"You mean, I'm not the only person in the world *you* could love."

I shrugged. "No. That's true, but it isn't what I meant." She nodded and I looked back at the bridge. It could easily be like a postcard picture—a symbol for the kinds of things we were trying to talk about. But it wasn't a postcard, it was a bridge, and I was suddenly embarrassed to be in the middle of saying the things I was saying to her. "We're just trying to make a decision," I said.

"I wish we weren't," she said.

"Wish away."

ANGEL ENDED up in an old house on the outskirts of the Haight district, living with four other people who never seemed to be around. Christmas Eve she was on the phone for hours with her family, who had all met at her mother's house for dinner. Angel wanted to be sure Debra had gotten their gifts right. From the sound of it, her conversation was mostly desperate—a lot of desperate explanations for what she was doing. But I was in another room, and when I asked her about it, Angel said I was wrong. She said she was just talking. There was nothing desperate about it. She was just telling them about San Francisco and how much she missed them.

"Do they know about me?" I asked.

"Not really. They know we came out together."

"So, what's the secret?" I asked.

"No secret—I'm still not sure what to say. So I'm not saying. Whenever you decide what you're going to do."

All the time we were together—this is how I remember it. I remember waiting outside department stores and boutiques while she was chasing down jobs, then eating big, cheap lunches so we could save on dinner, walking all over the city, and later jogging together at night in the park. She didn't want any short-term work that would end two days after Christmas. It was hard getting that across to employers. They would hire anyone for now, she said, but that did her no good in the long run.

Christmas Day everything stood still. We were in the financial district, just walking and looking at all the beautiful, abandoned glass towers, imagining how all the money and legal trouble in San Francisco was siphoned here every day, and how people got rich from it. There was very little traffic and almost no one around, except at the Hyatt, where there was some coming and going. This was the first time I asked Angel to explain herself, and why she had to be here. There was finally nothing to silence me or keep me distracted, only a lot of echoes wherever the city was empty. I said, "Why do you have to stay?"

"I don't have to. I want to," she said.

"Why?"

"Because, if we go back I know exactly what will happen. I never liked myself very much before, you know. Now that's changed, and I want to keep it—stay like I am—but I have to be here to do that. For now. It's so different."

"But I'm not staying," I said. This was the first time I had said this and been fairly certain it wasn't just a suggestion. She must have known. She looked at me, squinting and blinking, like she didn't recognize me.

"I'm not saying I want to be here forever," she said.

We were at the end of Market Street, looking back up the way we'd come, at the empty street. There was a lot of wind that day, and the clouds were moving so fast above the buildings that if I looked up it was easy to imagine everything bending and falling in, reverse vertigo making the straight angles swirl out of shape.

"This is it," I said. "This is what you want—a big, dazzling city. That's all."

Angel bit her lip and smiled, then shook her head.

"Maybe I'll visit. Maybe I'll come out—eventually."

"I hope you do."

"Then I probably won't," I said.

"That isn't funny," she said "Not at all. You don't have to convince me what a jerk you are."

"No," I said. "Then it's decided."

"But why?"

"I'm not going to stay just because you want me to. I don't have a better reason than that. I just can't."

We didn't buy gifts for each other. Either we forgot or decided without talking about it that there was no point. We ate leftovers, went to bed early, and watched reruns on TV until we were asleep.

When we had left Jolene's I was pretty sure that was the last time I would ever see her. She had said her good-bye to us early, while we were still in her bed, barely awake. I remember her standing there and answering questions, like whether we should change her sheets and where to leave the house key. I could see the thick veins in her wrists, and her nice loose fingers that I had once taken to have such meaning—to represent a connection she had with all the power of beauty in the world.

But once I'd made up my mind that I would not be staying with Angel in San Francisco I began thinking that

I had better see Jolene one last time. This was what I had come for, after all—to see Jolene—and I had no idea when I would be back. It was a few days before I managed to reach her. When I did, she said she was very surprised to hear from me, though I didn't think her voice really sounded like it. I told her what was happening with Angel, and before I could finish explaining why I had called she suggested a place we should meet, "Out in the open," she said, for sandwiches. We set the time and hung up immediately afterward, as if it were the only thing in the world I might have called for.

It was like walking into that game she and I used to play: "I'm in a little bakery in the Noe Valley, San Francisco. It's one of those chain-store bakeries called La Boulangerie. You haven't seen me in five years. When you walk in, you aren't even sure it's me sitting there. My back is to the door. I have on a long, black leather jacket and my hair is back in a pink terrycloth band. I'm alone, having my lunch. I lean to the side to look at something and you see it's really me. You think I look great, like one of those actresses who never wears out. My legs are crossed and my foot's going up and down. I'm very thin. What do you do?"

There were not many other people there, mostly ones and twos, businesspeople on their lunch breaks, eating hurriedly. I stood in the doorway looking at her a few minutes, thinking through the scenario as she might have described it and trying to decide if this was really some-thing I should do. Then I walked up behind her, put my hands on her shoulders and felt her relax. "Do I know you from somewhere?" I asked.

She laughed and put her sandwich back in the basket on the table in front of her, catching my hands in hers and squeezing them. She wiped some crumbs away from her mouth. She looked tired. Her eyes were bloodshot and seemed fractured inside, but I didn't think she was aware of looking like that. "I'm so glad you decided to do this," she said.

"So am I," I said, because for the moment I was. I went and sat across from her. The chairs we sat in were attached to the table and swiveled so you could get in and out, but they were attached too close and kept you sitting unnat-urally straight. "I told Angel I was just going for a walk. To think about things. I'm so confused." Jolene stared at me, not saying anything. I looked at my watch. "I don't have long."

"Mmm," she said. "Me too. My time's nearly up." She glanced at the service counter. "Go on and order some-thing."

I shook my head. "I don't want to eat. I just came to see you. God knows why."

"I know, actually."

"You do?"

"Sure. You're at the big crossroads. You have to check

your path with someone close who really knows you—
be sure you're making the right choice, or making any
choice at all. Not that there's anyone who can really help
you with that." She smiled. "But that's a whole other
story." She had a bite of her sandwich.

When she said that, I realized she was mostly right
and I had come here to talk. "God," I said, "what is it
about being out here in California that makes you feel
like anything in the world is okay to talk about?"

She gave me a look like I'd just said something I didn't
mean. "People are no different here than anywhere else in
the world, Charlie. It's you. You're the one who's going
through the changes and growing and opening up.
Things look different because *you're* different."

Then I told her everything I could about Angel, the
whole story of how we had met, and how much it both-
ered me now she had decided to stay here in San Francisco, because I couldn't see what was the best thing for
me to do. "I mean, I've got it so mixed up. I don't know
how to think for myself anymore," I said. "If I go, it's
because she's staying. If I stay it's because she isn't going."
I paused. "At this point my ticket's bought and paid for,
so what the hell. Am I stupid or what?"

Jolene shook her head emphatically. "Not at all. Just
be sure she doesn't drag you down with her. She's a com-
plicated girl."

"You think so?" I asked.

She nodded. "I wouldn't like her otherwise. Give it a while," she said. "Time. Remember—don't force labels onto anything, just let it be." She held her hands apart like she was casting a spell. "Love is not something you can plan."

This was no help, though I didn't tell her so.

"Anyway," she said. She glanced at her watch and made a face. "I have to go now."

"Yes," I said, and we both stood up.

"You'll do what's right, Charlie," she said. "Whatever it is, you'll find it; it'll be there waiting, the right thing for you."

I walked with her, uphill, as far as the bus stop on Twenty-second where I'd gotten off, most of the time feeling as if I couldn't quite fit in the air surrounding her. I kept up a stream of talk to keep her from forgetting why I was there. I told her about the trip out west and I told her about my mother—how despairing she had seemed to me the last time I saw her. My voice kept rattling back at me, full of unfamiliar words, and hollow laughs. It went around the people we passed and through the people who passed us.

For a while at the bus stop we hugged good-bye. Jolene had a white cotton scarf on under her jacket and I pushed that aside to kiss her neck. Either she didn't stop me because we were in public and she didn't want to make a scene or else she didn't mind. Her skin was no longer familiar to me—soft and fragile seeming and full of the smell of her hair. She sighed once, heavily, and we hung on that way for a while. Then we both straightened up at the same time and looked at each other as if something funny had just happened.

"Well," I said. "I won't keep you."

"No. I'm so glad we had the chance to do this."

"So am I."

She put her head to one side and smiled. I slipped two fingers in next to her cheek, underneath some hair that had blown across her mouth and pulled it away for her. "I'll try to stay in touch," she said. "Promise."

"Yes. Me too."

Now she was backing away from me, taking little backward steps. "*Ciao,*" she said.

"See you," I said.

It was a street corner like any other street corner in the world. There was a man standing next to me reading the newspaper. I looked at him and felt like nudging him, pointing at Jolene and saying something, like, "Hey. See her? That's my girlfriend. A woman I used to know. A very good friend of mine." He would nod and peer after Jolene, squinting because his eyesight wasn't good. I would say, "Funny how things turn out, isn't it?"

But I didn't say anything and he never looked up from his newspaper. I stared at him until I could begin to categorize a few things I thought of his face. He had delicate brown hair and a pointed nose and there was a brownish cast to his skin, which made it seem as if his jowls and the top of his forehead had been rubbed in ashes. He looked very sad, and it made me angry to see that, because there was also an undercurrent of righteousness to the sadness—a fighter's attitude that maybe came from having people always accuse him of being a mopey kind of guy. It turned the look of sadness to something sour, for me. Once in a while I've had the urge to hit a complete stranger, and this was one time.

I looked up and saw Jolene go across the street, all business. She stopped to wave at me in a burst of sunlight that nearly wiped her out. I waved back and she went around the corner and that is the last time I ever saw her.

A WEEK after that, I left. Angel and I waited together downstairs for the airport shuttle. It was just before six o'clock in the morning and she was barefoot, wearing sweatpants and a T-shirt. There were creases on the side of her face where she had slept on it.

"You and I, we're like a couple of kids together," I said.

"Don't say that," she said. She was leaning against me, with one foot up against her leg to keep it warm. "Right now there are only good things to remember," she said. She traded feet and leaned back against me, firmly, closing her eyes like she was going to sleep here now for a long time.

"I meant it in a good way. We've always had so much fun," I said.

"It was more compelling than that."

"Of course," I said.

Then the airport shuttle was there. Angel stood in the doorway until I'd found a seat. She waved at me, and I leaned in front of a musk-scented businessman and his newspaper to wave back. And for an hour or two after that I was conscious of all the things she did, as she did them, so my time was divided in the same increments as hers—jog for half an hour, shower, dress, eat, look for work, things like that. This was no kind of separation; I hadn't really gone anywhere. Then I was already halfway across the country it had taken us so long to cross, headed back where we'd come from, and I knew how much I was fooling myself.

There were things to take care of at home. I'd been in touch with my mother off and on while I was in California—once to tell her I had arrived safely, another time to say I wouldn't be back for Christmas, and in between that to let her know I was all right. She visited me just after I got back, and stayed with the Garcias in their spare room. I saw less of her than I had expected when she first called to say she would be coming down. She was always with the Garcias, talking about old times and having drinks, which was fine with me. I didn't think I had it in me to confront her with the things Jolene had told me. I wasn't sure that would accomplish anything, except to prove to her once and for all how little consideration—as she was always saying—I had for her. She might deny that she and Jolene had ever been more than friends, and I wouldn't know if she was telling the truth or not, or how to force more out of her.

Surprisingly, the last day of her visit we had a frank discussion about some of this, and I saw that she wasn't kidding herself about anything as much as I had suspected. She said Jolene had always had a wonderful way of including people in the way she saw herself. She said it was mesmerizing. Jolene had so much enthusiasm and insight, like she was a part of some other world that didn't last—where everyone was quick and friendly and witty, doing only important things—and she would always include you in that just by the way she treated you. She said it was hard to resist. But what she thought was at the center of it all was a real lack of self-knowledge. Jolene was a kind of illusion, even to herself, she said. Aren't we all, I wanted to say, but I didn't.

"One night, Jolene was at the house," she said. "I'd had too much to drink. So had she. You probably remember a few nights like that, don't you?"

I nodded. "A few," I said.

"The moon was out and there was a kind of a mist in the air that was so strange. It didn't seem to belong. It just hung there. Anyway, Jolene wanted to go outside. She said, 'Let's go outside and be wild women.' It was March, and all I could think was my feet are going to get soaked. I didn't want to go anywhere. But you know Jolene, once she had an idea in her head. So out we went."

She paused. "I can't remember exactly everything that happened that night. She wanted me to sing a song to the moon—'I see the moon and the moon sees me . . . ,' something like that. I thought she looked very nice singing it. Then we walked for a while. The road was pure white from the moonlight, like a film negative, and there was all that mist. You know what I mean. Where we ended up, I think it was at that park next to the old swimming place. Jolene wanted me to swear to something, I can't remember what, now. It had to do with a man I happened to like then. 'You will go up to him and say anything you want. Next time you see him. *Anything.*' Something like that. I honestly can't remember this terribly well. But the one thing I do remember—not that it's the most important thing in the world, she just kept on saying it—she said, 'Mary, this is your life. You won't be the one to cry when it's over.' That was it. I thought it was one of those defenseless, stupid things people say when they're all out of strategies, but at the same time I thought it also made sense." My mother stopped, pinching her lips between her fingers and blinking at me. At first I thought she was going to cry, then I saw she was laughing. "She could say a thing like that, you know, and it wouldn't sound completely crazy."

"Yes she could," I said.

"Anyway, that was Jolene."

THE REST of that winter I worked at a bookstore, where I made much less money than I had selling shirts. Angel and I were on the phone every other night at first, and there were weekly letters from her. I was surprised that the way she came across in those letters was not quite the way I remembered her. Her perspective was unfamiliar and had more irony in it than I'd expected. She told me about her new job, selling jewelry at a shop called Goldfarb's. The best time of the day, she said, was eating her lunch in the little park outside the Transamerica Pyramid, alone, on the stone steps that made her legs go to sleep if she sat too long. "It's the time to be with people and by myself." Often she'd bring a pen and a pad of paper, and that was when she'd write me. She said, "I feel so close to you here."

There was a point where things slowed down, late summer, and contact with Angel began to seem more like a chore than anything else. I wrote her something about that at the same time she did, and our letters crossed in the mail. Her letter said one thing: "This is the last time I have it in me to ask: When are you coming?" My letter said the other thing: "I think it's time we quit pretending this is ever going to amount to anything." I remember opening her letter there in the bookstore, standing between stacks of new self-help books by authors with last names from A to G. I had the dolly in front of me with two cartons of books from Viking on it, and my razor knife in one hand, ready to slash open the top of the box. I'd put off reading her letter all that afternoon because it felt so thin and hazardous. I really didn't know how she was going to say this, or how much I wanted to hear it.

Then some combination of cues finally set me off—the titles and jackets of some of the books I'd been shelving that day, like *Getting the Love You Need* and *Helping You: How to Help Others Help Yourself*, maybe, or maybe it was the smell of new books that I had come to associate with thinking about Angel all the time, and carrying on imaginary conversations with her while I worked here, going up and down the stepladder and listening to the soft classical music that was supposed to suggest a literary mood to book buyers. That was when I chose to open her letter instead of the box of books that was my job to open. I kept her letter in my pocket all the rest of that day, too, open, folded in with the book orders, so I could see it whenever I had to check off something newly arrived, damaged, or missing. And by the end of that day, I had decided my time without her was up. That was how I put it to her on the phone that night. I said, "I'm coming out."

"Charlie, there's a hundred other ways it could be."

"A hundred other ways to pretend," I said. "But only one that's right."

"I'm glad you're so sure," she said. We talked a little longer about the usual things—the weather, what we did at work, who we liked and who we didn't. Then at the end of the conversation she began to seem impatient. She said, "So, look, this is it. I don't want to hear from you again, unless it's in person. You don't know how hard that is to say, but I have to say it."

"I can imagine," I said.

It was a few weeks before I made it to California. I remember standing outside her door at the new place she had moved to. It was warm, just before dark, and I was trying to picture how this would begin—what she would say and what I would say back to her. I heard footsteps inside, someone she lived with running upstairs, and then from a room overhead a voice that was too muffled for me to make out. Next to the door was a panel of small windows, and through that I could see part of the hall-way inside, which was dark and littered with shoes. Lights were on at the end of the hall and I could see the bright yellow floor tiles in the kitchen, and the breakfast nook she had described for me in one of her letters. I saw her once, then again, going past the door with a knife in her hand. I waited for her to reappear, but she didn't.

Then, maybe because I had stood for so long on her front steps with a bag in one hand and nothing to do, I began thinking of a man I'd read about once. He had sprinkled kerosene all over the front of the house of a woman who had jilted him, set a match to it, and run. The end of that story has descriptions of the fire kissing the air, making black and orange lily streaks and sizzling as it burns through the outer layers of her house paint. Then the man runs down the main street of town, because he is so deranged by his actions. There he's caught by some men who always disliked him, carried away, and beaten and left out to die in a snowbank. "It's not funny, it's not funny," the man keeps saying to the men who are beating him, presumably because they are laughing so hard as they do it.

This was a true story and it had nothing to do with me, yet I was thinking of it. "Angel," I said, and knocked once on the door. "Angel!" And I waited, willing her to walk out past the doorway and into the hall where I could see her.